"This book settles in this Faulknerian way into its own Yoknapatawpha County. Lustre, Sharone, Destiny, Eddie, Pedro, all of these people live within the landscape of San Suerte."

Laleh Khadivi
author of *A Good Country*

NOMADIC PRESS

WWW.NOMADICPRESS.ORG

MISSON STATEMENT Through publications, events, and active community partici-pation, Nomadic Press collectively weaves together platforms for intentionally margin-alized voices to take their rightful place within the world of the written and spoken word. Through our limited means, we are simply attempting to help right the centuries' old violence and silencing that should never have occurred in the first place and build alliances and community partnerships with others who share a collective vision for a future far better than today.

INVITATIONS Nomadic Press wholeheartedly accepts invitations to read your work during our open reading period every year. To learn more or to extend an invitation, please visit: www.nomadicpress.org/invitations

DISTRIBUTION
Orders by teachers, libraries, trade bookstores, or wholesalers:

Nomadic Press Distribution
orders@nomadicpress.org
(510) 500-5162

Small Press Distribution
spd@spdbooks.org
(510) 524-1668 / (800) 869-7553

MASTHEAD

FOUNDING PUBLISHER
J. K. Fowler

**LEAD & ASSOCIATE
EDITOR**
Michaela Mullin

DESIGN
Jevohn Tyler Newsome

Lustre

Requests for permission to make copies of any part of the work should be sent to: info@nomadicpress.org.

This book was made possible by a loving community of chosen family and friends, old and new. For author questions or to book a reading at your bookstore, university/school, or alternative establishment, please send an email to info@nomadicpress.org.

Cover art by: b. Robert Moore (bybmoore.com)

Author portrait by Arthur Johnstone

Published by Nomadic Press, 1941 Jackson Street, Suite 20, Oakland, CA 94612
First printing, 2023

Library of Congress Cataloging-in-Publication Data

Title: *Lustre*
p. cm.

Summary: Taking place in the other California, the desert city of San Suerte, *Lustre* is about the luckless Lustre Little, a boy haunted by the violence of his hometown; ex-convict Sharone Bonilla, who is haunted by his history; and Destiny Deveraux, an orphan, come of age, who is learning and teaching love and responsibility.

[1. FICTION / African American & Black / General. 2. FICTION / Historical / African American & Black. 3. FICTION / Romance / African American & Black. 4. FICTION / General.]

LIBRARY OF CONGRESS CONTROL NUMBER: 2022947222
ISBN: 978-1-955239-45-5

LUSTRE

LUSTRE

KEENAN NORRIS

**NOMADIC
PRESS**

Oakland · Philadelphia · Xalapa

contents

foreword
>by Micheline Aharonian Marcom

introduction
>"We All Saw the Sun as God:
>A Conversation with Keenan Norris
>and Laleh Khadivi"

PRE-HISTORY	1
HISTORY	9
THE TRIANGLE	31
LUSTRE	53
SHARONE	57
HOME	81

reading guide

foreword

I grew up in the part of Los Angeles which wasn't L.A. proper, but suburbs we simply called "the Valley," ignoring or not-knowing valleys other than the San Fernando existed—the San Gabriel, for example, or farther out than that, myriad cities and towns that made up what is called the Greater Los Angeles Area. I don't recall when I first learned of the Inland Empire, but it was long after I'd left Southern California for the north of the state, and to this day is a place I've visited only a few times, mostly passing through on the way somewhere else. This place one "passes through," of four million people, with smog as the biggest complaint of its residents, and after that, bad traffic, is a world I've come to know primarily through the writing of Keenan Norris, who, in several books now, has made it his world for literature.

In the southern region of the Golden State there are certain realities familiar to almost all its residents: the hot sun that guides the days, the ubiquitous tall skinny palm trees dotting the streets and gardens, the coyotes and rattlesnakes that roam the open spaces, the dry Santa Ana winds that in the fall bring the hot air across the land, and the great mix of peoples who have immigrated from all over the U.S. and the world: Mexicans, Filipinos, Chinese, Koreans, Armenians, Ethiopians, Blacks, and whites—the list goes on. In Norris' dream-like, physical, sometimes gritty prose, in its dialogue so particular to the voices of his characters in this particular time and space—three African-Americans who call the imaginary town of San Suerte home—we get a snapshot of "a hard blasted city haunted by the Mojave...corroded by violence" and the intersection of three lives. Sharone, Destiny, and Lustre cross paths in one apartment-house, and each in his or her own way confront their pasts, face the challenges of their present—"chase revelation," as Norris calls it—in a city where "there [is] no good, no evil, just life and death." *Lustre* is not a book that offers false hopes or easy redemption, or even forgiveness for past transgressions; instead, it affords the kind of communication, and communion, that literature and reading make possible, whereby a place, and a people, based in part on those Norris knew growing up, find themselves fully imagined in a work of literature and brought to vivid life. Albert Camus once wrote that literary art should consider the balance of weighing itself down in reality, "so that it does not disappear into the clouds," or, on the contrary, "drag itself around in leaden shoes," and how each artist must find that balance "according to their sensitivities and abilities." Here, in Norris' imaginary city, in the oft passed-over Inland Empire, he finds and makes that beautiful balance.

MICHELINE AHARONIAN MARCOM
author of *The New American*
and *three apples fell from heaven*

introduction

We All Saw the Sun as God:

A Conversation with Keenan Norris and Laleh Khadivi

Keenan Norris: …There aren't a ton of people who write about the I.E. [Inland Empire]. That's why I've always wanted to write about it. It provides a point of origin. It's Southern California, and it retains some of the tarnished, scuffed-up sheen of Southern California. But it's also different. It's desert. There's a sort of austere beauty to the mountain ranges and the desert landscape that is a challenge to write about. I think it is an interesting place. Just the idea of writing about a place that is next to a famous place—

Laleh Khadivi: A famous storytelling place. How did San Suerte get you to *Lustre*? How did it get you to the characters in the book? To Destiny and to Sharone? How did San Suerte get you inside of their lives?

NORRIS: San Suerte is a fictional city in the real urban metropolis of the Inland Empire, which sits adjacent to Los Angeles County. The I.E.'s a lot Blacker than most of the rest of Southern California outside of L.A. A lot of Black L.A. moved to the Inland Empire. A lot of middle class Black people, like my family, moved there. There are also a lot of poor Black people—a lot more poor black people that moved out there, especially to San Bernardino. When I first wrote this story as a novel, it had several middle-class characters, but as a novella *Lustre* is basically about the folks who live in Suerte because they are poor and have no choice. I wanted to depict that landscape, the meeting of the rural ex-urban landscape with people coming from one of the most archetypal Black ghettos in the world: South Central Los Angeles. That was, you know, central in my imagination. It corresponded with a lot of people I knew growing up. A lot of the Black kids I grew up with not only were from South Central, but were living with extended family in the Inland Empire. A lot of them, whether middle class or underclass, were refugees of South Central's decay.

KHADIVI: Okay, so, the geography opened up to the various demographics of the characters in terms not of their ethnicity so much as how you arrived at your story. How, in a migration sense, did you get to this particular place? From what I know of San Bernardino—which is a little— it's inhospitable to human life.

NORRIS: True.

KHADIVI: It's not an oasis like Big Sur, where fish are jumping out of the river and landing in your lap. It is desert. And I think the indigenous first people had a sense of what to do to live on that land, but everything since then has been really artificial. Yet your characters are super organic. You know, they're organic of the most human-desire sense, but living in this kind of artificial setup. I couldn't help but wonder in this time where we have all these conversations about climate and environment, what about this landscape and the particular ways in which people have to create it, to make it livable—because of the heat, and a little because of the cold in the winter and the desolateness—what does that do to people who are formerly urban? Like, with Destiny, I just got the feeling of her desire to leave. Her name evokes it and her relationship to her environment and the people in the book evokes it. She's one foot out already. Is there something in that environment that while people ended up going there, people are also trying to get out?

NORRIS: Absolutely. A lot of the characters in the book are refugees of the urban space. There probably is a great kind of speculative fiction text to be written around the climate of that area—that kind of ground zero for global warming and record-breaking pollution... Everybody in the Inland Empire is from somewhere else. And everybody in California is from somewhere else—but, you know, there's this romance around Los Angeles, this romance around San Francisco that does not exist with the Inland Empire. Yet, four million people live there. It's what Gertrude Stein said about Oakland, right? "There's no there, there." But there are four million people there.

KHADIVI: Yeah.

NORRIS: And that's ultimately the root of the there, there.

KHADIVI: Yeah.

NORRIS: It's still under construction because the construction's not that of buildings and so forth—it's of history and culture.

KHADIVI: Yeah. And generations.

NORRIS: And just time, the sanction of time.

KHADIVI: I think about ways in which an author really has to build the whole house to write about a door knob. I feel like you built the whole house of San Suerte— the radio station, the churches, the murals, the landscape, the neighborhoods and the stories of the neighborhoods—just to let these four characters sort of rise into them. I had a question about the characters, though: How did you know that you wanted to be roving through your protagonist like that?

NORRIS: The book started out as a much larger book. It began in an omniscient third voice that told the story of the city itself. And over time and through many setbacks, I saw where the story was and where it wasn't, and I melted it down to what worked. So perhaps it does retain some qualities of the original, more epic design.

KHADIVI: Roving through multiple consciousnesses is hard for a novella, and yet, oddly, you pull it off. I think you did a really nice job of just giving us these snapshots. Deep, but thin, you know? Snapshots of these people's lives and their interrelations to each other... What is the relationship of Lustre in this novella form to your other fiction?

NORRIS: First of all, I always wanted to write a character named Lustre/Luster.

KHADIVI: Well, there you have it.

NORRIS: Yep. I always wanted to do this because Lustre comes from *The Sound and the Fury*. The boy in *The Sound and the Fury* who's just bored out of his mind. He's forced—he's conscripted, essentially, to be the caretaker for Benjy. And Luster's wildly creative and mischievous and he is the cause of all the trouble, including the wild scream of sound and fury at the end, which Benjy vents because Luster, in his boredom and mischievousness, drives the car the wrong way around the church— he drives the church route backwards. I wanted a character who, you know, was getting into shit, you know? A little hellion.

KHADIVI: He's gentle though— much gentler than the Luster of The Sound and the Fury.

NORRIS: That's true.

KHADIVI: He also doesn't have a Benjy.

NORRIS: Right.

KHADIVI: Except at the end—maybe a little hint. But for most of the book—

NORRIS: He's on his own. I also think I probably have a little more insight into Lustre/Luster than Faulkner did.

KHADIVI: Yeah?

NORRIS: I'm in his mind whereas Faulkner wasn't.

KHADIVI: Yeah, yeah. Faulkner had that long leash.

NORRIS: Right. But I always loved the fact that this old white man from Oxford, Mississippi had the insight to give a Black character the name Luster, because it's such a Black name, in all senses, yet I've never known a Black person with that name. It's like—it's brilliant. Until Raven Leilani came along, that name had never again been touched by our literature. This book was supposed to come out a couple months before hers, summer 2020, but it caught covid and now here we are.

KHADIVI: What about the notion of *luster* as shining? That a white man should look at a Black character and see not darkness, but light.

NORRIS: Yeah, and Faulkner is, you know, we're all limited in our experiences and our circumstances and by our era and so forth, but Faulkner is a brilliant writer who does what I think we all want to do, which is to, at least in moments, in passages of work, to escape ourselves.

KHADIVI: To hear like the gods, which I feel like he did.

NORRIS: Yes.

KHADIVI: So, this book settles in this Faulknerian way into its own Yoknapatawpha County. Lustre, Sharone, Destiny, Eddie, Pedro all of these people live within the landscape of this place, San Suerte, which is in your other work. Do you see these as one big work?

NORRIS: So my first novel, *Brother and the Dancer*, is set in the Inland Empire, but it's set on the borderline between the middle class and the underclass, with the one character, Erycha, being from a San Suerte sort of area, while her counterpart Touissant is from the middle class part of town. They are divided by a freeway. This was much more my experience of growing up there: Primarily middle class. Or, going from the one to the other, like, physically traveling from one to the other. Or dating somebody who was from the quote, unquote "other side of the tracks," or playing basketball in the hood. My dad worked downtown for the County Rehabilitation whatcha call it. He was a psychologist and he worked in rehab, reintegrating people into the workforce. There were also two black barbershops on opposite sides of the street— one on the same side as the County Rehabilitation and City Hall and all that, and the other facing it a few feet away on the other side. The one was full of gangster rap music and boisterous heathens who were never on time to your appointment. The other was full of gospel music, prim and proper people, barbers in full suits and ties and whatnot. There was also a black bookstore, Phenix Books, run by my first literary mentor, Faron Roberts, right next to the unholy barbershop. Faron introduced me to Omar Tyree, who has been a mentor for twenty years. He brought Toni Morrison and Kareem Abdul-Jabbar and many other prominent black writers of the era to town. Faron would tell me stories about growing up in Philly and having to cross gang territories to go to the library. He kept that black bookstore going throughout my entire youth. Right next to the bookstore was the mall, Carousel Mall, which has since been converted into a kind of social aid space. So I spent a lot of time down there. I had, like, a lot of interesting experiences there— many of them related to my father's clients.... [My family] was pretty solidly middle class. But San Bernardino, over the time that I lived there and since, has become much poorer to the point that for several years in the 2000s and 2010s it was the second poorest city in America, after Detroit. For a number of years... That downtown area was full of poverty, of madness, of criminal activity... So, yes, it formed in my imagination. I thought about ways that I could take those people and those stories and reform them into an emotional and imaginative truth.

KHADIVI: I think you are succeeding with that. So, this is a very revised book. When you set out to revise it, when you realized there were parts that didn't fit and it was gonna be shorter and you wanted to string together all the parts that were working for you, what did you want this book to do? What *do* you want it to do?

NORRIS: I think I want it to do two things. First, I want it to express Lustre's imagination.

KHADIVI: I do like the idea of a god consciousness in the form of a child.

NORRIS: Lustre sees the sun as the god figure, right? The sun is not just omnipresent, but so willful, so dictatorial over human designs in that space. Like, the sun is very bright here in the Bay Area where we sit, but it's not the same. It doesn't control your life in the way that it does in the I.E.

KHADIVI: Well, we all saw the sun as god. All the cultures did. The sun was always up there—how could it not be? You were, I can see, experimenting with the dramatic shapes a story can take.

NORRIS: Yeah, because the other thing I want the story to do, and this is part of what the god consciousness of the book meditates and revolves around, is the moral question of redemption— redemption for Sharone, given his past. Given his past, given his commitment to an internal redemption narrative and given his relationship with Destiny.

KHADIVI: I've read a lot of your work and it's been a great privilege because I'm a big fan of the place writers and you are a place writer. Where else do you want to write about?

NORRIS: *The Confession of Copeland Cane V* (Unnamed Press 2021) is set in East Oakland. *Chi Boy* (Mad Creek Books 2022) is mostly about Chicago. Can I ask you a question?

KHADIVI: Oh, sure.

NORRIS: What's the experience of reading a writer like me whose work is so place-specific to a specific area in America for someone like you whose work is so migratory, so international, so much about immigration and upheaval?

KHADIVI: It's a relief. It's a relief because the motivation for the drama, for the plot, is not movement. It's something else. The thing that makes all of my characters go is the need to go. And I think reading your work is to see the ways in which the characters have to move on something else. They have to move on tragedy. Or they have to move on desire. Or they have to move on ambition... About 25% of us are in motion all the time.

NORRIS: And the rest are not.

KHADIVI: The rest are not. Until they have to be.

Laleh Khadivi's debut novel, *The Age of Orphans*, received the Whiting Award for Fiction, the Barnes and Nobles Discover New Writers Award and an Emory Fiction Fellowship. Her debut documentary film *900 WOMEN* aired on A&E and premiered at the Human Rights Watch Film Festival. Her most recent novel is *A Good Country*. She is an Associate Dean at the University of San Francisco.

PRE-HISTORY

Lustre Little bent over the bathtub, spreading his khakis lengthwise across its still water. When one side of the tan pants had been saturated, heavy and blue, he lowered the khakis even deeper into the water until they were deep wet. He held the furthest edge of the right pant leg with one hand, the belt buckle with the other, the khakis perfectly suspended. He'd been washing his khakis like this for as long as he could remember. It was a delicate process, but one he had mastered. As long as the water soaked in slow and every inch was wetted, the system worked as proper as a washing machine.

Sharone Bonilla sat in his chair a few feet from Lustre, reading. He was probably the last person alive who still read the paper in the morning. Leaning forward, he stared at the *L. A. Times* headlines and tried to come alive with the dawn. "Y'all think y'all hard out here. Shoot, in Sudan you got kids in Jordan jerseys, flip-flops, totin damn AK-47s."

"Yeaaah, we gets it in." Lustre didn't look up from his work. The violence going on over there was of another world. Suerte had its own issues, plenty of them, and besides 6:30 in the a.m. was simply too early to go mixing the problems of Africans with African-Americans. Lustre kept his mind on his khakis.

This was the routine. Sharone's schedule was like rolling craps: 7 to 11 in the a.m. he worked a day job at the downtown bakery, then 7 to 11 in the p.m. he delivered pizzas in Suerte's North side suburbs and the exclusive ranch community in the hills above. Wedged in between, no siesta, the brother was busy with a day class at community college, stalking down that barber's license one unit at a time. Hard as it was, it wasn't the work itself that got to him, even though it throttled him out of bed in the mornings and numbed him into sleep at night; it was school that cut him like a blade, that forced him to hope, that filled his mind with a day-lit world.

At least he didn't have to work Friday nights anymore. Newer cats had come on who had to shoulder that burden. He could relax, do some chores, put the apartment in order. He folded up the paper, rubbed his fists against his closed eyelids, knocking away chunks of sleep, and laid free, slow eyes on the boy: Lustre's off him, too, Sharone thought, playing with the name. Lustrous too little. That's what happens when you change addresses more than clothes, that fabric gives itself a rest, starts to hang off of you. It loses its creases and peels away like from an orange, leaving you in your boxers in the cold-ass morning.

The boy lifted his khakis from the bathtub water. Sharone got up from his chair and drained the tub. He headed for the kitchen, sliding across cold tiles, past the dining table, to the stove. Lustre followed after Sharone with the dripping slacks held lengthwise in his hands. When Sharone made it to the stove and turned on the four burners, Lustre held his khakis over the low red-blue flames. The boy had a finger slipped in each belt buckle and was holding only the top end of the right and left pant legs above the leaping fire of the stove flames made all the more lively by the window Sharone had opened and the hard Santa Ana wind that drove into the apartment. The stove flames danced in the gusts as youngblood moved the wet khakis back and forth delicately, patiently, letting them dry in the heat. After a few minutes, he turned up the flame. Sharone grunted, remembering, as he did every morning, how all his South Central uncles used to starch and iron better than the fussiest woman, until they could stand their slacks stalk still against a corner wall like a ghost was wearing them. *What'chu know bout that starch job, boy, what'chu know bout that?* they'd hoot and holler.

It took hours to make pants do that and back in the day it had amazed, not bothered him; but now even Lustre's brief routine was trying his patience.

"Why don't you do this before you go to bed?" He was figuring the time things would take and wondering if he'd be late to work yet again. "E'rything's process," he lectured. "I'm prepared come morning, gots my garments ready already."

"That don't work for me." Lustre shrugged; indignant and harassed. He hit his foot hard against the carpet in four-four time and hummed to himself. He remembered singing mornings in a sunlit kitchen when he was still his mother's baby, when he was still truly little: How her pretty voice mingled with Prince's to "Black Sweat" and "The Beautiful Ones" and "Somewhere Here on Earth". How he would flow in singing the falsetto parts even higher than she could. That was before she gave birth to his sister. And before their father died. Looking out the open window and across the way, Lustre saw two big, barrel-chested, African men in snow white linens and a third, smaller man, Eddie Richard, whose clothes matched his clay-colored complexion, huddled together. The men stood in the G Street strip mall parking lot. Behind them, the nail shop and the Chinese take-out had let their doors open prematurely; CLOSED window signs still hung like early morning moons in their doorways.

Sharone had left the kitchen, went back to the bathroom and returned with his chair. He was a minute moving the sleeping bag that lay at the foot of the kitchen table out of the way, folding it up small and putting it in its proper place before he sat down.

"What they needin from the nail shop?" Lustre wondered out loud. "Plus," the boy kept on, his curiosity breaking through, "what's

Eddie even doin out here, showin his face?"

Sharone shrugged. It was none of his business, or Lustre's. "You heard about Paid? The Mexican kid who people say Eddie shot?"

"The boy alive, right?" Sharone asked.

Lustre nodded. "He's my friend. Eddie put him in a halo."

"E'rything ain't what it seem, youngblood. Eddie might not even been the nigga behind the trigger. You cain't jus go believin the rumors people put in the street."

"Like they got for dogs when they get hit by cars," Lustre said, contemplating neck braces and furniture. "When they survive. Upside down lampshade lookin thing."

Lustre ticked his tongue along his teeth. He stared out the window at the San Suerte sun, glaring goldenly even at this early hour. Later, it would be very hot. The sun had a life of its own in the desert. By noon it would sit in state, a mean sweltering living god. Lustre imagined it holding in its hot grip each soul in the city, deciding daily what to do with them, who would live, who would die.

"Paid's home now. Cain't move his head for nothin, though." Lustre turned down the flames and rotated the tan khakis over them once more before turning the burners off for good. He had been shivering in his boxers for a long time now. The minutes were getting short. It was time to go to school or whatnot.

Outside, Lustre noticed that the crew had got ghost and in the place where they had posted themselves now stood a sign reading NO LOITERING. He followed Sharone to the bus stop.

"You actually gon' go to school this time, cousin?" Sharone pressed him.

Lustre considered lying. But what was the point? He trusted Sharone enough to tell him the truth. He shrugged at the question like it was water he could let run down his shoulders. He leaned against an available light pole. "Nah," he finally answered, and looked down the gridded, intersecting roads, the palm trees tilting in the wind like so many dollar store statues. "It's bout to be summertime. Ain't no reason now, school almost out. Too late to change my grades now." Then he heard the bus coming, its deafening, arthritic brakes sounding as it made the turn onto G Street and slowed gradually to a stop. He began to edge back from the waiting crowd and away from Sharone. Sharone wasn't watching him; his attention was taken by a listless girl on the opposite side of the street. The girl's clothes were tight on her and her frame ran away five ways with each step she took.

"Hey, is Des home?" Lustre asked.

"Nah." Sharone said over his shoulder. "Destiny at work in the morning. Cleanin house. Domesticatin." Without looking at Lustre, he motioned toward the hills, the ranch, the clientele up there.

"When is she gonna come home?"

"Not my business. I don't know her schedule like that." Sharone's words were drowned out by the approaching bus. He had already begun to board its stairs before he could take his eyes off the ebb and flow of the girl across the way long enough to notice that his little man was no longer right behind him, but had instead cut back the way they'd come and was jogging down G Street with what looked, at a distance, like a handful of grass, but that Sharone figured was money out his mother's purse.

HISTORY

The white Thunderbird skidded out of control and off rain slick Central Avenue and kept on skidding till it met violently with an unforgiving factory wall. Sharone's mother was killed and Sharone was orphaned by the impact. That was 1982. Sharone was three years old. Now that he was twenty-seven, he no longer thought about and barely even remembered the explosion that woke him in his car seat, the shearing metal or his sister's screams. His brain was a petty scrap collector, the bed of his pickup brimming over with excesses of memory, like so many sheets of metal and beams of iron burdening it; too much had come to pass, too many things had happened in the intervening years to hold and remember. For instance, the direct aftermath had included him and his sister being handed over to their emergency guardians, his grand-dad and grand-dad's latest girlfriend. Sharone still remembered the woman by name, though her name only reminded him of pain and damage. Sharone's brain held memories as randomly as it lost them. The woman had run off with a white man, or moved to Florida, or both, and after that it was just him and his grand-dad in San Suerte.

When he was eight, Sharone wandered out past the developed housing tracts and the dry river gulch into the desert and killed the rattlesnake that went for his ankle when he mistakenly stumbled over it. He felt its fang glance across his ankle bone and the long tendon next to it. He leapt at the snake, grabbing its throat, pinning it to the ground. With his free hand, he dug his house key out his pocket and punctured the snake's airway. The afternoon was staggeringly bright, the kind of day when the sun could peel a boy's skin like a fruit. He knew the rattler could have killed him, or at least severed his Achilles with one good clean strike. But he had killed it instead, saving himself. The desert was his garden and in it there was no good, no evil, just life and death. He waited with the rattler until the moon came up and the coyotes started to call, their voices half sad, half desiring prey. The desert moon always comes early, he reminded himself. But the dark couldn't be too far behind. He carried the snake back home to show the old man what he, but a child, had done. That was the second time he almost died.

Years later, a police officer would shoot at him on Crenshaw Boulevard. A girlfriend would lie on him that he had beaten her and paid gangbangers to kick in his apartment door where he was staying off Slauson. The boys pinned him to the ground and made him deepthroat a glock until the gun barrel almost asphyxiated him. He remembered, later, after they were gone, looking out at the astral plane of night, like cat eyes studying him in the dark, prowling him from above. His eventual arrest on drug possession charges would be followed by a bad ride with the police wherein the arresting officers turned off Long Beach Boulevard and down into the Lynwood cuts. They parked the car on a side street known for gang-active Mexican cats and on this day them eses scattered around corners and over fences as soon as the siren sounded and the police car made its appearance. The only person who did not run was a helpless slumped drunk. The officers beat that old man more deeply into his unconsciousness to impress upon Sharone the necessity of confession.

You got the complexion for the forced confession for the coerced collection, his cellmate riffed the next day in jail. And, sure enough, his partners used a homegirl to front their drug money and hired a real honest to God private attorney: All that man had to do was put on a suit and collect a check and say "officer misconduct" for the charges to disappear.

Sharone took that good turn for what it wasn't, a sign that his boys would always have his back. The trust that it cultivated and the fact that he had to pay them back for the legal fees only served to solidify him deeper in their world. He settled into life with a girlfriend. Sharone would always remember their last night together. "I'ma be back in a minute," he told her. "Jus gotta take care some things."

He didn't know how untrue those words would be. Years later, coming and going from a different apartment in a different town with a different girl, this one named Destiny, he would be at pains not just not to lie to her, but not to promise more to her than the moment. He remembered leaving, closing the bedroom door so fast it nicked his heels and then locking the apartment door behind him and forgetting to check it even once. Down the cheese-grater stair steps and out to his car, he hurried. He had some dealing needed doing, some money needed making over on Long Beach Boulevard. But it never did get done, or the business did him instead of the other way around, because later that night on the boulevard, Sharone was arrested for the last time.

By then, most of the brothers that had put money down on the private attorney for his prior were behind bars themselves. Sharone knew he was lost and didn't even trouble with the public pretender the state assigned to him, instead giving up the ghost of his freedom in interrogation. For the plea agreement, he was sentenced to seven months in shock incarceration boot camp.

When he did finally come back to the world, it was in San Suerte, where not much had changed: The apartment house was the same as he'd left it, his grand-dad was still wanting him to get a legal tax-paying job, Suerte was still the hard blasted city haunted by the Mojave, raked by Santa Ana winds, corroded by violence. But at least here he had his grand-dad; at least here he had a home that meant more than a rent check. He realized now that the real reason he felt so different had nothing to do with Suerte or L.A., but was instead internal: Sharone felt urgency in things where he never had before, a certain something inside him that tolled like a bell reminding him that his every action might be his last and his final definition.

Back at the apartment, his grand-dad shook his rigid hand and took a kind tone with him, lauding his return, telling Sharone he was more than happy to house him. Sharone noticed the dead and hardened skin along the old man's reedy hands, the moles springing up like moss on a tree; an old tree, a living body being retaken by nature one bit of bark at a time.

"You know what y'all need in jail," his grand-dad shared programmatically, "it's mandatory remedial classes in e'rything. And if you pass those classes then you gotta do all the college classes mandatory, too, all the way up to Quantum Physics. That should be the sentence. Then either e'rybody or nobody will be in the pen!"

Sharone thought that actually made a strange kind of sense. But he wasn't thinking about jail anymore. He was home now. He would never go back. He let his grand-dad say his piece, quietly nodding at each word. Then he let himself feel how tired he was and excused himself and he went to his room, where he slept very deeply. When he woke it was to the old man hammering home two nails to hang a photograph on a hallway wall. In the photograph everything was green and wet, seemingly connected by streams of jungle dew, the environment of some far-away world that at first he fantasized might be the Amazon or somewhere else very exotic. Then he noticed the inscription at the bottom of the photo: *Columbia River Gorge, Oregon, USA*. Why there? Why somewhere so far? Sharone wondered. The man in the picture posed beneath a semi-circle of impossibly tall trees. He leaned against a rock that was jagged but rounded along its underside while its upper half was flat as a fade haircut, sheared that way by some natural force strong enough to cut a boulder in two. It took a moment for him to realize that the man in the picture was his grand-dad. Like the first man alive, he stood in his Eden, having come flush and new into an experience of the earth. He was so much younger than Sharone had ever seen him before, with a slender face and a chest and shoulders as thin as mountain air, but he posed over that big rock like a God who had sawed it in half himself.

"Sooner or later, gotta go search things out for yourself," his grand-dad hollered in the hallway. "Cain't just wait for God to come and give you a calling. Gotta go find it!"

It struck him that his only real journey had been to jail. There were possibilities, opportunities that he had, at basic, failed to imagine. His lack of imagination, he realized, was the root of his problem. Before he said a word to his grand-dad about his future plans, Sharone was building mentally, thinking up goals and piecing them together. Right there with the picture staring him straight and true, the urgency came upon him; an awakened moment as real as any threat on his life—he knew he should become of value to someone other than himself before he was so old and unrecognizable that even a mirror wouldn't tell him much—a degree, he figured, a certification or license, and a profession, that would be a start. He thought about becoming a barber and having his own shops. That first day home, he sat down with the old man to talk out his future. Now he had a plan: A loading job at a local store, a GED at Valley College, then a barber's license. Given some time, he could have a chair at a barbershop anywhere in Cali. His grand-dad approved, but told him he needed to read and to think more than he needed a license to cut heads.

"Cain't be half-steppin your way outta hell, Sharone!"

They were standing right beneath the loud rush of the whole-house-fan. His grand-dad preferred it to conventional air conditioning, but you couldn't even place loose papers anywhere in the apartment when the machine was going full-tilt lest they go flying like flocks of birds. Let alone the noise, which left Sharone only catching parts of what he was being told. "The soul needs buildin-up," the old man counseled. "Needs repair." The rest was just a wordless air blast that made him shiver.

"Your ears will adjust," his grand-dad hollered from two feet away. "That electric bill ain't no joke!"

Fair enough, Sharone figured, because he had little choice but to agree.

When night came, the fan was finally silenced and the whole apartment house went quiet. The only thing that wouldn't go to sleep was his mind. Sharone couldn't stay put for anything. He took a walk. He asked around. He scared up a loaner bicycle and then just rode and rode. A gentle, weak rain sprinkled him and eventually the dawn shed its first rose-red blood upon the sky. As was usually the case back in the day, he was high as the mountains and even in first light the trees still had the sinister aura of prison guards, powerful and immovable. He rode into a lighted alleyway wedged between the Federal Bank and the DMV. There, he rolled one last spliff on his bicycle seat and closed his eyes. His mind went foggy. He had lost all tolerance for THC. The image of a tall, thin, knife-shaped woman, her black hair ripping with the wind rose up in his mind. They met eyes and she came his way. He placed his hands on the blades of her shoulders and then, stunned, watched as her clothes fell from her, each article leafing off and winding away supernaturally.

Sharone dropped the spliff onto the wet ground and opened his eyes. His fantasy was a passive one and, befitting that, he came to, to a world unchanged. He hadn't made like Rip Van Whatever and slept for a thousand years. Nobody had a gun to his head or a hand in his pocket. But on the other hand, he wasn't any the better for smoking, even as good it still felt to fly away like that. He allowed himself one last spliff and this time when he drew the smoke in and closed his eyes there was no juvenile dream: He was seeing his terrible baptism and his first sin there in the grip of the spliff. Under the light of an inescapable moon, he was a child flailing away in an unrelenting rain-fall of blood and he neither felt responsible for it nor able to remove himself from it. It was the car crash that killed his parents, it was the first time he sold angel dust hand to hand, knowing it wasn't weed, wasn't coke, but insanity instead, and it was the worst memory of all, the memory that would have him seeing ghosts one morning while trying to get Lustre to school: The girl in the L.A. dopehouse who had come in off the track asking for a pimp— he stopped his mind before it went further.

Between the Federal Bank and the DMV, Sharone studied the skyline. The streetlight that had at first illuminated the alleyway died in spasmodic flickers crackling weakly out of existence. He looked down at his feet, where he had dreamt of blood coating the sidewalk but where, instead, little pools of rain formed in the pavement divots like so many stilled streams. He swept the blunt guts off the bicycle seat and rolled one last, last spliff.

In the morning, he found himself at the barbershop. Music broke from the sub-woofer and three 12-inch speakers roosted on shelves in each corner of the shop. First, he heard the light suggestion of the organ; its first chords a sort of second birth where he had come into his childhood in Los Angeles Baptist churches. There was anger and fear and guilt and remonstrance and wisdom and care in those vanished place marks. The choral melody emerged, rising, lovely and full-bodied, so intimate he imagined the entire choir was waiting in the barbershop's back-room behind a closed door. Then, suddenly, a succession of sonorous bells intervened, replacing the flawed voices, opening out the rhythm like a cracked and blessed vessel that could touch its most perfect form only for a moment. Then the song wandered toward its finale, silence, the bells tolling, tolling, on toward silence.

The music gone, if only for a minute, the barbershop's casual cacophony welled up: Yes, a course the crazy lady can use the ladies room, ain't nobody turned away in this house. Some sassy-ass been diggin in what'shisface-movie star's pockets for diamonds and gold. Mr. Morgan wife gonna nag him all the way to the ER, 'n even if the Lord up 'n put all this land under liquidation again, she'a nag him underwater. It's a female God forever 'n bad times for a brother.

"Haircut," Sharone addressed the nearest barber. "You can take it down low and fade it in the back."

"Right, right." The barber nodded. He took a minute to eye Sharone's overgrown natural at a distance. Then he called across the shop, "Jess!" At the far end of the shop, in a corner shadowed by a high mantle, Sharone saw a thin, dark-skinned, tautly wound woman raise her head and rise from her knees. She'd been at work scrubbing between the floorboards so there were soapsuds between her fingers. She rose and washed her hands, tied her wild black hair into a bun, and started across the shop towards them. She looked at Sharone with shining eyes that probably glowed when the clock struck midnight.

The next song began, plunging ahead organ first.

She smiled broadly and led Sharone to an open chair. She cradled his head in her hands. "Jess isn't my actual name, if you was wondering."

"What you wanna be called?"

"Ms. Little." She moved her hand gently along his head until it felt kind as a kiss.

He fell asleep—there was no drowse, no space of half-consciousness; he was dead in his sleep. And his sleep was cavernous. It had dark facets, ruptures in the unconscious which were not dreams, and down he plunged, knowing nothing but that nothingness. And when he awoke, his scalp and face were baby-bare; he had arrived newly clean. Ms. Little anointed his head in the age-old burning rum solution that had always brought tears to his eyes, but that cleansed him now.

She saw he was awake and handed him a mirror. He looked at hisself.

"You like it, or is it just decent?"

"You're good," he admitted. "I should be payin you extra, but I cain't. I'm broke as a joke." Impulsively, he reached up and held her hands in his own. "You know, I used to want to be a barber," he confided to her.

She wriggled her hands free from his and suddenly he could see in the mirror those hands on her hips in an indignant pose. "*Used to? Like you still cain't?*"

"I don't know if I can."

"Don't know if you can?"

He nodded at her but hesitated at the challenge her question posed.

"You can," she concluded with some force.

He rummaged in his deep-sewn pockets and produced twelve crisp dollar bills, the standard fee. He handed it to her.

She handed it back to him: "Nah, I'm not a stylist. No license. I cain't accept money for this."

He paused, money in hand. He was confused. In the near distance, he could hear the song's discrete interlude, a cluster of chimes. She took the money from him, folded it neatly and tucked it back in his pocket. "C'mon, haircut's over. Raise up, let's give the dead some life. I'll walk you out."

He acceded to her will, or whatever hand it was that guided him. Outside, the parade was over. The final celebrations had crescendoed, echoed and vanished. Debris littered E. Someone had thieved his bicycle. A skin-and-bones junkie went about collecting soda cans in a black trash bag. The *Radisson Inn's* pink and beige Bell Tower tolled the new hour. "That bell," Ms. Little said. "I wanna walk with you, but I cain't; gotta be back inside." She looked up at the giant clock face, her eyes the color of midnight, "There's things need to get done." Sharone looked skyward, too, chasing revelation.

A week later, he went on a late night walk that took him to parts of town where no one ever was robbed. Police cars rolled up alongside him three separate times to ask where he was going and what he had robbed and Sharone turned out his pockets and after the third time he turned around and went home. It was round midnight when he made it home. He opened the door to the apartment house and a leaf of lettuce hurtled through the air, slicing past him an inch from his ear. Sharone dropped his closest companion in the doorway and looked back to where the flying food had fallen on the walkway outside. It was white and under-ripe. The whole-house-fan bellowed louder than ever. The rule was to only run it during day hours, but now it roared at night. Inside, the old man's papers and things were winging around the dark apartment in a dizzying aerial array: What looked like the electric bill and some Triple-A ads and Kodak photographs from way back, as well as the morning newspaper were all airborne like so many kites released to the wind. A business card came knifing toward him through the cluttered dark and he had to dodge fast to avoid being cut. Then another came and he threw up a hand and caught it: Martinez Tailoring, he read as he battled the mess of flying papers and made his way to the main room, and then there Sharone saw him, at the center of the chaos, his grand-dad dead.

The man's lifeless body respected gravity far better than anything else in the apartment, including Sharone, who felt light-bodied and liable to fly away his damn self. He gripped the edge of the couch where his grand-dad sat dead. Everything inside him exited, all muscle, all bone and blood. The apartment swirled above him. The old man was dead and the world had taken wing and all Sharone could think was, *Why is it I'm not flyin? Why is it he cain't fly?*

After the funeral, Sharone returned to the apartment. When he looked at the framed picture in the hallway, his grand-dad had become a ghost. He had disappeared from the physical but was still hovering there spiritually in the hallway. Sharone could feel him at his side, and far from being fearful, it was a comfort. Now in the framed photograph he saw his parents on a calm, warm Los Angeles night holding each other arm-in-arm as they posed on the Central Avenue sidewalk. Behind them loomed the façade of a factory that no longer existed. Sharone wondered how big the factory must have been and what in the world could have killed it. His parents were smiling widely, genuinely in that captured moment. Whatever had separated them later did not exist in that flashing instant.

Both were wearing what looked like newly shined dancing shoes. Sharone figured that just past the factory must have been one of the black nightclubs that Central used to be famous for but that had disappeared around the time of his birth, with the 80s and the end of the good life along that stretch just south of downtown. Then his parents disappeared, ghosted from view, and joined him, invisible presences at his shoulder. Then he saw himself in the photograph. He was the final ghost. He saw himself in a closed casket, six men bearing him to a plot of broken ground beside the space that held his parents.

He cried, then, for the first time since his incarceration. He found himself staring at a spoon, a door, a felled palm frond in dead moments that threatened to become hours if he did not do something, if he could not claim his place amongst living beings.

Sharone took the picture down from the wall and put it in a box and put that box in another box and then stored the thing where he wouldn't have to be reminded of its several ghosts daily. He knew that as long as he was alive and they all were gone across, he would need to take some living ownership of this apartment. It was his grand-dad's place, of course. There was no getting around the debt that he owed a dead man over and above the rent he paid. But he needed, at least, to spiritually sub-let his space.

He went further; favoring air conditioning over the giant fan. He subtracted all the blues and jazz records from the massive, old living room shelf and stored them in a common space next to, on top of, underneath all the other tenants' things. The only visible reminder of his grandfather was the oak-walled record player that still dominated the small living room, but of course without records in the apartment it sat in silence and disuse. Destiny had bought a Snoop Dogg album on vinyl once, but Sharone wasn't interested in music about violence and whoring, so it, too, ended up stored up.

His grand-dad's things were almost all hidden in that common space. What wasn't hidden in the common space was placed out of view within the apartment house itself, a packet of letters sent to Sharone while incarcerated, now stacked neatly in a corner on a high shelf in the kitchen, the pin-up poster of an old movie star tucked beneath the television, a .45 and a rusted box full of bullets wrapped in tin foil and stashed in the cupboard beneath the sink. Sharone hadn't completely erased the old man from his life, but he had reserved for him a separate cove and in doing that had put him away and made a necessary break into his own new life.

People had noticed his changes, too, and credited him for it in the form of trust and requested service. Destiny noticed. Ms. Little noticed.

Yes, worn out Ms. Little leaned on him hard. With the weight that she bore on her back, Sharone couldn't blame the woman for begging off some of her responsibilities and asking him to help carry her load. If nothing else, the lady would tell you exactly what was on her mind, no sugarcoat. He remembered their most recent meeting, which was really a solo performance, with him serving as the audience: "I got two babies, Sharone, and no degrees, and no husband here to help. They say all men leave, but that ain't true. Some is taken. Mines was taken. I used to be angry at him for dying, angry at his doctors and at my God for allowing it.

"Men can smell loss on a woman. Did you know that, Sharone? Take it from a single woman— I know. I know y'all know us by the way y'all cast y'all eyes down and the way y'all shoulders fall and y'all sadness when your eyes look close at us. Women, we don't know nothin but love once we're in it. But men, y'all ain't never at rest. I won't include present company: Maybe you're different, I'll allow.

But most men is only awake to what they can get from the woman, what they can get from every woman. That's just how it is. I knew my man was liable to wander, liable to temptation, but I always knew he would come back home. I knew he would raise his son. And then he was gone. And now here I am, still here somehow with these two children, this creeping pain won't leave me be and this life still to live. I done thought this through every which way to Sunday, Sharone. Been down on my knees in prayer. Been studied the bible backward and forward and what I learnt, Sharone, is that sisters like me is Hagar: You remember Hagar? Sarah's servant, Abraham's other woman. We're put here to do what the Sarahs won't accommodate theyself to, whether that be cleaning or cooking or screwing or raising a man's child after him and everyone else including the Lord done left us. I stopped reading the bible and I stopped praying and I stopped believing in God because what God would allow this? And then, like God had been waiting till he broke me down to godless dust just to build me back up in the strength of the Spirit, here you come, Sharone, not no sometimey lover, not no womanizing, ain't-shit-liar, but a man, a man for my boy. I don't know what's on God's mind. I don't know about His plans for me, but I believe that He sent you to us, Sharone."

"I'ma do my best," he heard himself say.

"My Lustre needs you."

Praise, praise, Sharone thought, like an old church lady who waves her fan in front of her face and closes her eyes and hopes for the best. Not that Ms. Little was very old nor at all simpleminded, for she was neither. But the simple core of her needs shook his dungeon. He could not say no to her, not when it came to Lustre. Sharone had come late to his responsibilities, but late was not never, so when he arrived they all were waiting for him, more of them than he knew could exist. What rationale was there besides not being man enough

22

to house a child? Why not add that obligation to the others he suddenly carried? Sharone's obligations ran deeply in many rough directions. Sometimes he imagined his goals and dreams and his obligations and even the past he left behind all coming into collision, like when cars careen headlong into one another, flesh and bones wedged in between the severed metal. His imagination could get ugly that way. But, of course, real life had never been no beauty queen.

Sharone gazed at his keloid-colored face in the *Seafood & Pizza* bathroom mirror: lookin like forty miles 'a bad road, he thought. As ugly as everything else in this town. Age and wear were setting in in the form of keloid scars and wrinkles rising along what had been a smooth, penny-colored face. In a year or two, he would look bad and broken-down as the shops along his delivery route, shut down and ceding to the dirt. The only face in Suerte worth looking at far as he was concerned was Destiny's. Acne cratered her left cheek like so many red freckles drawn deep into the skin. Her mixed heritage went in waves across the rest of her face, different shades, like so many shadows and moments of dim light. Most of Suerte's sons and daughters were mixed some-way or other, Sharone included, but usually the face just chose sides. It was black or it was brown or it was creole or it was Chinese or Filipino or white. On no one had he ever seen their whole heritage like he saw the generations of relations on Destiny's face. At first, he had thought it was a trick of the halogen lamps in the apartment. Or maybe that his eyes were going bad along with the rest of his body. But that was not the case. He could still see a girl's hips switch back and forth a block away. He replaced the lightbulbs the first time they flickered. Destiny was just different, at least on the outside.

He came home, quietly shed his clothes, and went straight to the shower where he stayed washing himself until every last speck of his work was scrubbed away. There were no clean towels, no towels, in fact, that hadn't been used three times twice over by both him and Destiny so instead he went into the main room and let the warm night dry his body. Whenever he looked down the corridor that led past his bedroom to the end of the hall, he would notice the slightly open door into the girl's bedroom and have to remind himself that he was naked and that opening her door would be the worst idea in the world.

After his grand-dad's passing, Sharone had put the second bed up for sale and had it off his hands for a hundred dollars. He never imagined that he would need a bed other than the one he slept in himself. It hadn't occurred to him that there would be a woman living in his house whom he wouldn't sleep next to in the same bed, not to mention the additional company of a child addicted to running away from his mother's apartment who also was in need of sleeping arrangements. Once again, it had been a failure of imagination on Sharone's part: Destiny had shown up one day, and Lustre never really left for long. Now, Sharone slept on the couch some nights, on the floor others.

Just when he had done everything that needed doing and he was ready for sleep, he heard the doorbell's high, tinny ring. It was Lustre. Sharone knew his ring. He went to open the door and checked his watch as he did so: 11:30, not too late.

At eighteen, the only living situation Destiny could afford out of her own pocket was a room in the home of a schoolteacher who sub-let to her because Destiny was cute and naïve and might make a good green-card bride for her nephew in Manila, who was trying to get back into America permanently. "He looks nice, no?" the teacher would implore. "He wouldn't care if you kept all your boyfriends." Destiny was a rookie at renting, but even she knew not to pawn herself off that easy.

After that ordeal, she shacked up with an old lady whose mind had flown its coop some time before. There were many eccentricities with that woman, but Destiny remembered the overalls she wore and the yellow sun bonnet she sported to stave off heat stroke as she tended the same plot of soil in her backyard each day, raising dirt and roots in the name of gardening. When she wasn't digging holes, she was listening to doo-wop cranked to full blast while she talked over the music to Destiny about back in the day. "White people were fucked up, girl. I tell ya, they'd come straight out, call you a nigger and the whole nine yards and not give a gotdamn. You could respect that, because at least you knew where you stood. I liked those times. I was born in Savannah. White man said to me, 'I don't like what I'm lookin at.' I said 'Well, I don't *know what* I'm lookin at! You look like a rabid dog. I'm beautiful, chocolate beautiful.' And I was beautiful back then, God as my witness. I can be a little prejudiced, though. He wadn't but so ugly. That was 1955 or 56 or 67. E'rybody just told you straight back then. None of this transvestitism. I don't know how you found that Eddie, what with all these pussyfootin men scared of they own shadow. I had a cousin got hooked on heroin. 1950. 60, maybe."

Destiny rode that one out a good long while, much longer than she should have. Eventually, her boyfriend left her and she came to her senses enough to do some leaving of her own. The search continued.

Living with Sharone, she found, was a totally different, saner world. Coming home most days, she could hear the sausages crackling goodness on the stove. Whenever she ate his food, Destiny would tell him how he should quit his jobs and drop out of school, move to Beverly Hills or San Francisco or somewhere else where people's dinners cost more than her rent check so that he could become a chef and get rich. Sharone knew that line cooks, which was where he would more likely end up, were barely getting by, but it was still nice to hear her talk to him like that. Besides, he would remind her, San Suerte was where the McDonald's corporation was founded— Genesis being a vacant lot now overgrown with weeds and cracked car parts, memorialized by a two-foot tall worn, wooden placard that explained about the man who conceived the great world-wide operation. "Fast food's cookin, too," Sharone liked to say, simple as sunshine, just so he could nudge her a little, just so she would keep the easy warm banter going. "This where it all started."

"Oh, please," Destiny came back on cue. "McDonald's is a claim to shame, not fame, Sharone, and you know it. Niggas love a Big Mac more than sex, I swear."

In her room now, she remembered that he had made her bed. Destiny lay on top of the folded covers so as not to upset his design and she stared up at his peeling ceiling. It was a good thing he was so nice to her, and so clean about his things in general. Destiny scoured the dirt out of deep corners in vast houses for a living, but she couldn't tidy and clean her own room any more than she could make herself dinner. Things stayed messy where she laid her head. Maybe that was why Sharone had given her his bedroom, to keep the rest of the apartment respectable.

"You in the house, Des? You ready to eat, or was that a ghost done floated in?"

She emerged, called, self-consciously running her hands through her perm. Her hair was unruly to begin with and lying down just bruised her perm up all the worse. She wanted to look right when Sharon was around so she made quickly for the bathroom to look herself over before coming lightly into the kitchen. "Hey, Sharone."

"Hey, Des." He placed his half-melted, half-rusted spatula on the kitchen counter. "It's food on the table." He did something proper with his hands that directed her eyes toward a plate of garnished salad, plantains and seasoned pork. He'd drawn her chair out for her, too.

"Thank you, Sharone."

"That enough for you? I know you been workin all day."

"As if you haven't been doing the exact same." Destiny went on talking, not about work but about other things, things she would buy with her paychecks, shoes she wanted to see, hairstyles she wanted for her head. She liked that even when she carried the conversation away from his intended targets, Sharone would stay listening. Most men, if she was living under their roof, would want to rule everything from the conversations on up to her body— but not Sharone. She came to the subject of love. "You know how dudes think, Sharone. I'm still figuring that out. I don't wanna come off bitchy or not approachable in the way I carry myself. But I want a man's respect. As a woman, it's difficult to gain a man's respect. And if you have his respect, it's difficult for him to desire you." She paused, played with her fork and the food he'd made for her. "I was messing around with this player dude, I won't lie. But I think, now, I want someone solid who has balance and some values and whatnot."

"Wadn't under the impression you cared what any man thought, let alone what I think bout men thinkin bout you."

"Well," she said, "I guess I do."

Sharone met her eyes for a moment. Then he finished his food and went about the apartment getting his keys, his wallet, his belt.

THE TRIANGLE

Destiny came out of her bedroom with her day clothes hugged to her chest. She had on matching pajamas because a couple years back she had got it in her head that matching pajamas were a status symbol, or a sign you were home-trained, or something like that. The top always seemed to fall off one shoulder. The bottoms had started a campaign of cat scratches along her legs. The whole outfit was becoming annoying so a lot of nights she just wore some old shorts and one of Sharone's billowing T-shirts. They had become familiar enough that she could do this without him saying boo about it. But they weren't having sex and they definitely weren't a couple so it was one of those delicate things where it was acceptable as long as it was between them and no one else knew; if somebody came knocking at the door and she was wearing his clothes she would slip away into her room to change into the matching pajamas.

Coming out of her room now, Destiny was surprised not to see Ms. Little's boy. It was normal for her to wake up mornings and find Lustre asleep on Sharone's couch and Sharone asleep on the floor. Destiny figured if Ms. Little wanted a man to help raise her son, she could do worse than Sharone. Usually, Sharone would walk the child home in the morning and help get him ready for school. Only the other day, Thursday, Friday, one of them weekdays, Lustre had been right there, wide awake, watching cartoons. She knew he needed to get to school, but she hadn't pressed him too hard on it, just a word or two in that direction on her way out the door. After all, it wasn't like she had been an immaculate student herself. Destiny'd spent one year in the same city public school system that Lustre was struggling through now. For years, she had begged her people, that is, her six-figure-salary extended family who had taken custody of her to keep her out of foster care, to let her go to public school. When she finally got fed up with her classmates at the private Catholic school that they put her in mistaking her for a white person and telling her that the five other black kids in the school looked like monkeys and felons and her grades started to slip, the family finally relented, placing her in a program that bussed privileged children to the city school. That beget her sophomore term, when she ended up getting almost straight A's and felt very good about herself, despite knowing that it was hard not to do well in classes that moved so slow because the teachers had to repeat everything multiple times—San Suerte's schools having declared themselves the nation's sole multi-dialect district with sensitivities toward Spanish, Tagalog and Ebonics, as well as the core English requirements. The ranch kids were only there to improve the test scores so that the school wouldn't be taken over by the state.

Most of the public school kids were like Lustre, truant, indifferent; it didn't matter what language you taught them when they didn't give a fuck to begin with. The test scores rose and the school remained independent and the program was discontinued. Destiny went back to the Catholic dungeon and waited to graduate. She remembered missing the public school. Easy grades aside, the public kids, when they actually showed for class, were so much more chaotic and artistic and alive than the children of Aquinas. She didn't understand how a boy like Lustre could hate school so much when the classes were easy, the girls were thick, everyone was a character and the sports teams always won.

Lustre was a curious little problem to solve, but someone else would have to do the solving. Destiny had other things needing doing. By the time she was out the shower and dressed, she was already running late for the bus. She hurried up G, past the elementary school and the government-owned homes and the blacktop basketball half-courts with their pretzel-bent rims. She was almost to her destination when she heard "*Destiny! Des, girl, what's goin on?*" She knew the voice immediately. It had no manners, just wildness running through it. Eddie Richard, with a fat cigar held loosely in his teeth, came dancing out of nowhere. She stopped and stared at him: She had no idea where he had appeared from, how she hadn't seen him coming. Destiny figured, not sadly, that he pretty much had her trapped.

He sprang up to her in a wild jester movement and cleared her right off her feet, one arm underneath her knees, the other holding her under her ass, his arms a virtual pedestal beneath her. He held her at eye-level and she noticed that his breath wafted sweet and dry, like so many hot, honeyed candies fresh out the box. "Hey, girl, it's been so long!" She breathed in his smell and wanted to kiss him. She let him hold her. For a moment, she reigned royally in his arms and then she felt his grasp giving and she whispered to put her down. "You look good, Des," he said, sighing.

"What's going on with you, Mr. Hustler? That's the real question." She was back on the ground now.

He took the cigar out of his mouth and regarded her. "Been doin my suave underdog, girl."

"Oh, really? What's that mean, Mr. Underdog?"

"I got plans for days, Des."

"Well, brother man," she said, regaining her sense of strength and self-purpose despite the shock and random sudden curiosity at Eddie's appearance, "what about those plans was so fuckin needful you just up and left me like you did?"

She knew he didn't have a good answer for her question and didn't let herself wait for what she knew would not come. He was talking but she wasn't listening. Her thoughts ran to his neck. She reached for it and ran her fingers along its thin, narrow length. Yes, it was still there, the risen scar tissue from the blue "C" tattoo that he had had removed from his neck.

"You can keep that up if you want to, now. Best massage I done had in a long time." He laughed, rocking himself back and forth. "It's gone, like you always wanted it gone. You was right, Des, cain't do no legit business with that mess tatted on me."

His teeth glinted a sunlit smile. She tried her best to resist him, the way he drew her like a hard directionless wind into his influence. "Good. That's real good, Eddie. I need to get to work, though. You have this way about you, where you just appear right in front of me, like outta nowhere. How do you even do that, is what I wanna know? Where did you come from? Anyway, this woman I work for, old girl don't hardly wait. Just hands me the key, then she's out."

He nodded. "Right, right. Gotta get that paper." He looked away from her, down the road where the bus was barely visible but gutted along loud as their voices standing next to one another. "Shit soundin like a airplane bout to lift off," Eddie mumbled. Then he smiled again and giggled kind of girlishly. She remembered that about him, too. Eddie was the strangest, stupidest, loveliest boy she had ever known. He was creative and persuasive and attractive, and that right there, all those enticing qualities running together inside him, was exactly why she couldn't let herself get too close. She had needed him gone every second that he was away despite the way her body ached at his absence. Missing Eddie had taught Destiny that all pain was not terrible. Without him around to distract her from herself, she had grown into her mind and body. She'd become more than the little girl half-created by his interest in her. She knew, despite the way her body responded to him, wanting to touch him, wanting to be held, that she needed to hold a line between them.

"I really do need to get going," she insisted.

Eddie was smart; he knew when not to press too hard. "Of course, of course," he allowed. "Like I said, I understand: I feels you, strong black woman. I ain't tryna block no hustle. But, listen here, I'm not runnin these streets like I used to. I'ma make sure we do sit down like grown folks, talk, get to know each other again. You still got that same phone number?"

She nodded.

The bus arrived.

"I'ma make sure," he promised.

The homes she tended were part of the same ranch development where her extended family lived, at the opposite end of the reserve nestled between open fields where tremendous chestnut-coated horses grazed. The whole reserve was a magnate's land holding, parsed out in small plots to the upper middle class. Destiny's clientele were residents of the ranch, the worst being the Huynhs, who owned a real-actual dinner bell that was suspended above the stove, with blue beads hanging down its sides. The mother clanged it to call the family to dinner; however, the bell was really Mr. Huynh's property. He banged it with sticks, forks, knives, the yellow pages, whatever he had his hands on at the time. He rang it for everyone, children, wife, Destiny; and everyone came when called. It would have been insubordinate not to. The best client was the Rincons, who either owned or rented (Destiny wasn't sure one way or the other) an impressive two-story. The man of the McMansion was Mr. Rincon, a retired Air Force officer. Mr. Rincon had slicked back his hair like a Hollywood

Italian don. He dressed like he had a GQ photoshoot to get to and carried himself like it, too. But he did not condescend to her.

It had only taken a ten-minute interview for him to hire her. Then he and his wife showed her around their labyrinth home, making a point to mention that Destiny should never ever dust the Diego Rivera paintings, but that the same did not hold for their picture-framed photographs of themselves and their two sons and a niece that now lived with them.

"My niece Perla," Mr. Rincon sighed. "Her mother was imprisoned." He looked at Destiny meaningfully. "The conspiracy charge is a scheme to put as many brown mothers in prison as possible. They have these bad boyfriends who sell drugs, you know? Then the prosecutor gets this line of guys and one girl. All the guys snitch on each other, but the girl who doesn't know anything about anything except she thinks she's in love doesn't say shit and ends up with a ten-year sentence. All the guys walk in one or two. It's ridiculous."

Destiny's mother was Portuguese, or Mexican, Destiny was not for sure which, or maybe it was both, but it was all one now: Dead was dead. The woman was fair-skinned, Destiny knew that. And she also knew that not being brown had not saved her mother. Magarida had been sent to prison for failing to dime on her man. In the end, they both went in and Magarida died there, behind bars, leaving her daughter an orphan. So now Destiny wanted to say, I know, I know. But then she thought how Mr. Rincon and his wife might be like her own extended family, throwing their last name on the girl and making her their reclamation cause, like they were right there with Jesus and the saints for keeping her in food and clothes and shelter. She imagined an involved heart-to-heart with the Rincon girl, where she would introduce herself and then the girl would tell Destiny that her name was Miracle, or whatever the Spanish word for Miracle was.

She would say how she'd given the name to herself when she turned eighteen to signify what a miracle it was that she survived her trials and tribulations. That was how she would put it, even though she was Mexican and Mexicans never said trials and tribulations. Then Destiny would respond with something kind, something intimate, maybe, "I went through the same exact thing. I know how it feels, that moment when it first hits, when you know the woman who gave birth to you is never gonna come home."

In actuality, Perla turned out to be fourteen years old and she hadn't been immediately orphaned the way Destiny had been. Perla's mother had gone away when Perla was ten years old. Perla knew what her mother looked like and what she liked to cook and how she danced and what gifts she wanted for her birthday and Christmas. Perla's mother wasn't a low-bottom dope fiend. By all accounts, she wasn't even an irresponsible parent aside from the drug charge. Perla didn't miss her mother, though. She didn't miss her because she didn't miss the neighborhood in San Suerte where she had had to live before the criminal case. Her memory crowded her mother into the memory of the neighborhood and the girl was willing to let go of the one to escape the other. Perla also didn't miss her public school. She had no hatred for Catholic school. In fact, she seemed to like the hard morality, the dogma, the discipline, which disappointed Destiny.

"What's your boyfriend like?" Perla asked Destiny, eschewing the sad stuff.

Destiny was in the girl's bedroom dusting her bookshelves. "I don't have one," she grated.

"What was your last boyfriend like?" the girl tried again.

"Never had one."

"Never?"

"Nah. Never. You have one or somethin?"

"Uh-uh."

"OK, then. They get to be too much trouble. Don't bother with it, at least not for now."   Destiny was surprised at the hard line her advice took on teenage romantic relations.

"That's what my auntie-mom says. Is that why you don't date, because your mom told you not to?"

Destiny wanted to clarify the difference between having a boyfriend and dating, but then she thought how what she had done with Eddie might not count as dating either. She wasn't sure what she and Eddie had been other than unlabeled lovers. "My momma never told me a thing," she shared. "She been in jail for years." She hesitated for a beat, still desiring the discussion Perla was all too happy to have with her but that she actually resisted out of some strange reaction to the happy girl. "How bout we play a game, Pearls? You ask me a question, I ask you one, you ask me another question, I ask you another one, so on and so on. How's that sound?"

"Have you ever had sex?" Perla asked.

That was when Destiny offered too much about her sexual history. She told the girl too much, virginity, how to keep it, how to lose it all at once or a little at a time. Eddie: She remembered Eddie undressing her. She remembered matching his hungry mouth, wanting him like she'd never wanted anyone. It had been like this each time they had gone to bed together and yet each time he had stopped himself and stopped her somewhere short of sex, preserving a kind of open untouched reservation in their relationship. With him, it was always her first hour on earth when all she needed was to be held. Then they finally did have sex and she remembered many things about it, almost all of it wonderful, but what stayed with her now was not the sex but how he had drawn back from her right before he entered her, how he had poised to come into her and then he did not for a very long moment, and that something about his hesitation told her that he was leaving for a long time—not that moment, but in the morning. She remembered, too, that in that hesitating moment she wanted to but could not see the left side of his neck because of the way his head was turned or because the room and the night were all so dark, so she pulled toward him and drew her tongue along the "C" for "Crip" tattooed there, that risen sliver of skin that she imagined had a texture and taste all its own. Like poison, blue poison, colored death. She had no idea what it was, but she knew then he had good reason to get ghost. She remembered feeling that ghost and kissing him anyway, parting his lips with hers and running her tongue into his mouth and directing him down to her breasts, between her legs, where she shuddered, first in fear, then orgasm, then fear again.

And when she woke, she felt his absence before she opened her eyes.

Destiny oiled the oak cabinets upstairs and moved downstairs, running her rag along the stairwell railing as she went. Perla had homework to do. This grown folks sadness was too deep for a child anyway. No sense in talking all day about it. Like talking to the wind and the trees and the sun about things that had happened and could not now be changed. And, anyway, the Rincon house took forever to clean.

After work, Destiny took the bus back from the ranch reserve to G Street. She found herself wondering if Sharone had come home before her, arranging wagers in her mind on who would beat whom home. And when she walked in the door clearly having won, she was surprised how disappointed she felt. She showered and put on different clothes and considered doing something different with her hair, she wasn't sure what, and all the while she was waiting for him without realizing that that was actually the only thing she was doing.

She heard his keys go clink in the doorknob and the hinges of the door cry open.

"Hi, Sharone."

"What's up," he called back, in that way people asked how she was doing without caring what the answer was. It was a little insulting to be wrapped in such a mental tangle over him and over men in general and have this man not even half-notice her. Sharone acted like this was just another greeting on just another day, though in fact it wasn't. Eddie was back: Her nightmare and her dream were here.

She came out of the bedroom and made her way to the kitchen where he was. "How was your day?" she asked.

Sharone, who was at the stove watching a pot of water boil, shrugged. "Ain't over. Still gotta work tonight. Pro'ly get a visit from the lil wanderer, too." He sighed and she noticed his shoulders sunk low and the whole architecture of his body fallen to a lazy posture like a run-down house. She could tell he didn't want to talk, but felt obligated now that she'd come into the kitchen. Destiny wasn't even sure why she wanted his conversation, considering all the trouble talking to people inevitably brought with it. "Was he around this morning, when you got up?" Sharone asked, still staring at his rice. "You want some of this?"

"Nah, I'm good. Thank you, though. Does his momma control him at all, that's what I want to know?"

"Not for me to say what their relationship is or isn't. I do know he be hangin out on the corners way too much, though. It ain't safe. That's where all the riff-raff be, drug dealers, hookers." The water began to bubble over in the pot on the stove. "You sure you don't want none a this, girl?"

He took the pot over to the sink and poured the water out. She came closer to him and looked over his shoulder. The rice was fluffy and dry and steaming warm. "Yeaaah, sure," she kind of purred and conceded. She went and got two plates, one for each of them.

"You know, that old man, old Hanh, owns that La Raza Liquor store? Which is strange, but whatever," Destiny began. "People know his reputation, but the story I heard is just all kinds of wrong: A couple weeks back, who was it, that Medea girl told me how she was walking past minding her own business while he was out sweeping, mopping, whatever on the sidewalk outside his door. Then she accidentally, accidentally mind you, stepped on his foot. Cuz you know how he goes around barefoot in the summertime. Anyway, that man up and smacked her booty!"

"What did Medea do?" Sharone wanted to know.

"She was shocked. She had never been slapped on her butt by no strange man."

"You don't know that."

"You bad, Sharone."

"I'm just sayin."

"So then, according to Medea, the man starts screaming on her. Not the other way around, mind you. He ain't apologizing for nothing. He acts like he's the one who's been wronged. He calls her ignorant. Says she don't know what poor is, what it is to struggle. He knows Xin-jang poverty, real Third World suffering, whatever the hell that means. But his two children, they both go to college in America, they both get a good education in America. Hahns started poor in China, but there wouldn't be no idiots left in America if America was full of Hahns."

"So what she do then?" Sharone asked. A smile had spread across his mouth, sad at its edges. He doubted the truth of the story, figuring Medea was either putting some fiction on whatever really happened in the liquor store or she was out and out lying to Destiny, getting a backdoor laugh at the expense of the new girl in the neighborhood, innocent yellowbone bird flying toward whatever folks told her. "What she say she did about it?"

"Didn't do a thing."

"Guess he taught her to be more considerate then." Sharone ticked his tongue against his teeth.

"I guess you could say that. You wouldn't catch no Portuguese people screaming on us like that, though. It ain't Catholic. It's hella outta pocket, I'm sorry. I'm pretty sure you wouldn't care to get your butt slapped by some old man, Sharone."

Sharone loved the silliness of these conversations. When he let himself wish for things, he wished their back and forth would last forever. This is the good part, he thought, trying to stay in the moment, in the flow of words, in the ecstatic leaps of her laughter. "Nah, nah. I'm not sayin homegirl don't have a right to be mad. You cain't just be smackin a female like that, least not in America."

"Especially not in the hood in America!" Destiny exclaimed. "I'm wondering what deal that man's made with the devil that no one's ever retaliated."

"You know how we are. We talk like we gon' put someone in the cemetery, but on the real we ain't tryna do a damn thing. Old Hanh just sound like he get it how he livin." Sharone shook his head.

Destiny giggled high and happy and went into the cabinet nearest her: "We still have cinnamon, or do I need to go to the store?"

"A lil to the right."

She fished around in the cupboards. Over her shoulder, she said "I might as well get in my pajamas since I'm in for the night." She brought the cinnamon back and sprinkled it on their buttered rice, mixed it in with a spoon: Poor people dinner. Sharone had taught her the recipe.

"Now, D girl, you tryna mock me? I was out last night, I gotta head to work in a minute, 'n you here talkin bout matchin pajamas."

"That's why I love you, Sharone. You're so much stronger than me." She settled back into her seat and for a long minute they just sat there, happy with one another.

"Well, if Lustre come round fore I get home, please be strong for me. Walk that boy back to his momma's cuz I am not strong enough to sleep on the floor another night. OK?"

"I feel bad for Ms. Little. It seems she just kind of lost him. I guess she's chalking it up to God?"

"I cain't call it. I don't know. I need to talk to her." The weight of obligation had re-entered his voice. He carried it sturdy where she bent under complication and stress. "I need to leave now," he said, staring at his rice again.

"A'right," came her resigned response.

She took his unfinished bowl of rice for him, walked it to the refrigerator.

In her dream, Sharone brotha-leaned in the doorway of the bedroom, his shirt off and his broad, deep chest rocky with muscles. His face was intense, especially his eyes, which stared blackly into hers, their softer, browner shades shadowed somehow. She was lying there, in half-sleeping repose, and in the dream she could see herself silhouetted soft and dark olive with hair white as moonlight. They came together, halfway between bed and doorway. He kissed her, hungry for her. She wanted him not just inside her, but disturbing the core of her, breaking all the peace and stillness she held onto, taking it from her, taking her and fucking her from out of one being and into another.

She woke to herself shaking. Coming to, she remembered like an ambition unmet and uncontained, her dream of him. The red flash of an airplane light broke past her window. Slowly, the dream receded.

Its vivid color and warmth fell away. The red light stuttered out of sight and the night's muted black and mild cool came back. It was another dry, windless day. She felt a lack, something missing from her thoughts and from her bed now that she had returned to reality. She wanted the dream back, or, if that was impossible, at least someone breathing to stave off the loneliness. But no one was home. And all of a sudden waking had become loneliness; she felt it inside and all around her and the only thing that seemed like it might stand in for a friend or good sleep was a deep warm high. She got her weed and paper from where she hid it and rolled a spliff on the bed and went and opened the bedroom window.

The best thing about being high wasn't that her problems disappeared; they didn't. She was as aware of herself as ever, but she no longer cared that she was aware. At first, she smoked by the window, directing her exhales outside. Then, after a while, she thought, Fuck, ain't like Sharone ever comes in here anyway, and closed the window and started pacing around the room letting the weed smoke stay in like a trusted friend. Spreading the love, the weedhead white kids liked to say. She laughed, remembering the whiteboy from the Catholic school with the Bob Marley stickers on his backpack who first put her on to the ganja and gave her his blown glass bong with the purple and red swooshes and swirls. The boy had had a crush on her and liked to give her things. Eddie hadn't given her shit but money and dick and a little bit of his time. And he didn't believe Bob Marley was any more special than he himself was. No woman, no cry, Des? Eddie would object: What kinda nonsense is that? No women, I'ma cry me a river, girl.

When she let the smoke out, it misted like the rolling fogs that never came far enough inland for her to witness. She wanted to see the water again; how long had it been since she had seen the ocean, swam in it, let it take her under in its brief dream? She wanted another brief dream, another fast escape.

It was late when she again awoke. Sharone had finally come home. She heard the shower water running. She looked around and noticed that she wasn't in her bed. She had fallen asleep on the floor, on Sharone's old throw rug. She rolled over and felt at her left cheek: the borderlines of Nigeria, Sierra Leone and Ghana imprinted where her face had fallen into the rug's fabric. She got up giggling, stumbling toward the bed. Her head and torso made it to the mattress but the rest of her remained floor-bound. The room was no longer filled with smoke, but now the lingering smell was the familiar after-scent of marijuana, like feet and oregano, half stench, half sweet. Shit, she thought. Shit. What if Sharone sniffs this?

She flailed up to standing and wobbled over to the window and opened it again. She hung her head out mouth open, tongue licking the night air. She tasted the heat and exhaust fumes, tire rubber and barbecue smoke, everything that flew out there in the darkness invisible. The night eclipsed everything, the mountains, the houses, the apartments, the barrio, the food-birthing fields, the vacant lots, the shuttered storefronts, the check-cash, the Mission, the Party Doll bar, with its black and white graffiti of Elvis and Marilyn Monroe, the Seventh Day Adventist steeple. Anything, anyone, surely Lustre, she thought, could get lost in this kinda night, this kinda dark.

She heard the shower water shut off and Sharone grunt in the bathroom. She gazed over at the digital clock on her nightstand: 2AM. What had kept him out so late? She knew he only worked seven to eleven; why had it taken him two hours to get home, conservatively, assuming his shower was a very long one? She ticked through the possible reasons in her head, from a flat tire on the public transit coming home, to a mugging between the bus stop and the apartments. She thought through less dramatic possibilities, too, like if the man on graveyard shift had called in sick and Sharone had had to cover his hours. It was the kind of thing Sharone was charitable enough to do, but she knew how closely he had to guard his sleep in order to get up and out in the morning. How many times he had cut off conversations with her in order to shower and go to bed. *Why you out so late tonight?* It was a lover's question, one she scolded herself for even having in her head because they weren't that. She wasn't in love with Sharone any more than she was in love with Eddie. But she wanted both them niggas; that was the truth. For different reasons and different parts of both, but both most definitely. She wanted what she knew she shouldn't. Not only men but the Westside itself, which was nothing to play with, she wanted like she wanted lovely broken black men. She was in love with this place, as dirty and dangerous as it was. In love with it just like being in love with a bad nigga. She wished her life had never made her leave this dim little place to begin with. Destiny did not remember her mother. Not a single detail of her. But she still believed that the months that she had spent with the woman, living in her arms, at her breast, before the conspiracy charges, was the best she had ever had it. It had to be. It couldn't be no other way.

They called the Westside the Black Triangle, white people did, because that was where the blacks had always lived. Where the off-ramps to the 10, 15 and 215 freeways let out at Del Rosa Avenue, Baseline and Second Street and formed an enclosure. The triangle wasn't really a triangle if you looked at it on a map or just knew the streets well enough. It had curves and breaks and sprawling warehouses in the way, messing up, redirecting what otherwise would have been triangular. But the whites had wanted to trap the blacks, she figured, so they did so by design by naming the ghetto and bounding it with the freeways. She was glad that they did it, too. The longer Destiny spent away from the ranch and in the triangle that did not quite triangulate, the more she wished its lines were even sharper, thicker and blacker.

She took off her pajama top and picked through her strewn clothes for the floppy T-shirt Sharone had lent her. Her breasts, unsuspended, fell and shook and trembled like the frightened children she hadn't birthed. There was no way of controlling them once they were out of the bra. Now they were out wandering around, disobeying authority. She was glad she had no real children to chase after like Ms. Little did. The loose, unregulated wisps of her hair fell independent of her perm, dripping down her face and onto her breasts. She could see the black roots coming back, edging in where her highlights were giving way.

She heard the television come on in the main room and the beat from a music video begin to thump: Some hip-hop song. Sharone didn't even like hip-hop. She had tried to meet him halfway on that by bringing home a Snoop Dogg record he could play on his granddad's old record player but he just waited till she wasn't looking and put it in the common space with all the other tenants' junk. Destiny hadn't taken it personally; she had just taken it as a hint not to buy him anything else and a confirmation that he really wasn't kidding when he said he no longer listened to rap music.

She listened from bed as the song played and the show went to commercial. The commercial was a preacher sermonizing about the evil of being promiscuous, how the wanton were asking for it, AIDS, TB, insufficient funds. Meanwhile, a heavenly scroll with his "checks payable" address ran ticker-tape style at the bottom of the screen.

She figured the television happened to be tuned to the last channel Lustre had been watching that morning, BET. Sharone was always saying how the only things BET showed were booty-shaking videos and Bibleizing hustlers getting everyone but themselves to praise and worship. It was like Fat Tuesday and then Ash Wednesday and then Fat Tuesday and back to Ash Wednesday, in everlasting paradox.

Destiny didn't know what was wrong with that, but she knew Sharone said he hated it. He wasn't changing the channel. She imagined him sitting there staring into the screen like a man looking down a long road leading nowhere and she wondered what it was about tonight that had him acting so different.

She sniffed around her room and decided the weed smell was safely out. She got up and went into the main room.

His bedsheets cloaked his body, but he was sitting up on the couch eyes open and alert. He stared up at her. "Late night for you, too?"

"You're listening to that show hella high."

"Oh, my bad." He turned the volume down. "My bad. Did I wake you?"

"Nah, not really. I've been in and out, in and out."

"Of sleep?"

"Of sleep." She nodded. "I was just wondering if anything was wrong, why you were still up so late, seeing as you have to get up early in the morning. I don't need to get up early, but you do."

Sharone didn't answer immediately. The show came back on. A girl danced around in a white wig and high boots.   "What do you call it, Sharone? The sex industry. That's it right there. What?" She stopped talking for a second. "You don't wanna talk?" she asked, innocent of the obvious. "What is it, Sharone?"

"Estrella," he said, pronouncing the L's.

"It's Es-trey-ya. You're talking about Ms. Little's daughter? What happened to her now?"

"That means star, right?"

"Yeah, in Spanish. In Portuguese, too."

"I just was thinkin bout those names, star and shine. She wanted her babies to be brilliant."

"At least the girl isn't being brilliant by running the streets. Where is Lustre, anyway? Somebody needs to reign his ass in."

"That's me who need to do that, I guess. It's why I got home so late. Ms. Little, ol girl been steady callin me, askin me to look for her boy. She don't have the slightest idea where he went to."

"So you went lookin for him?"

Sharone nodded. "Yes, ma'am."

"You're a good man, Sharone."

"Nah. Jus a nigga done slept too long."

"So, you couldn't find him?"

He shook his head and cinched his lips into a corkscrew frown. "It's the second time I seen someone, this girl, got me distracted. Ain't think Lustre was so liable to jus dash off like he did."

"So he was with you?"

He shook his head like he was trying to shake out some thought or memory. "The boy in the wind. He jus like to roam, I guess."

"Who's this girl that's got you flustered all of a sudden?"

"Ain't nobody."

Destiny studied him a second. "Ms. Little must be on the verge of a heart attack. I know I would be."

"She scared, she scared. And it's my fault, no doubt. But I talked to her and reasoned things out and settled her down some. What I figure is, Lustre went runnin loose, pro'ly thought to his self, 'I'm tired a Sharone's snorin ass. I ain't sleepin near that nasally nigga no mo nights.' I bet you anything he jus over a friend's place."

"What friend?"

"That I have no idea of. Lustre will roam town all day if he get a mind to. He know all the streets, buildings and children in this city. I know Lustre, though. That boy, he'll be fine."

Destiny glanced at the clock on the VCR. It was now 3AM and Sharone was still as wide awake as she was. She stood again. This time he didn't ask her to sit back down. He stared at the television and the preacher. She lingered above him, knowing how unimpressive she must seem in his shirt and her poorly done hair. She knew she was avoiding something almost inevitable between them. She felt the certainty that was Sharone inside of her like a bell tolling deeply, darkly. Destiny said goodnight and Sharone nodded at her and said the same. She went back to her bedroom and placed her hand, palm flat and open, out the window where she could feel the unmoved air, still with its heat, and she looked out on the stellar dimensions, the night, the stars, the worlds beyond this world, and she knew she was no longer a child.

LUSTRE

It did not matter where in the world Lustre was; he was in his mind inside a chamber that admitted no escape. The chamber was a shell and the shell was a closed circle. Thoughts came to him, pressed him with the powder residue and dead smoke stench of explosion and release. He knew death: His father was gone, which he had yet to truly, harshly look at in the face and underneath the face, below the skin and beneath the surface of himself. He could only come to his father through others, through boys and men whose lives had exploded, who were picking up the pieces or who were the pieces on the ground.

Something had detonated in his mind and in that rupture everything, right then, right there, was born and the history of all happening was recorded just like that. He was small to begin with, but the detonation revealed a universe inside which he was so little and his little Suerte world was itself no more than knee-high to a waterbug. The sun alone rose huge and godlike. And even the sun, when he looked at it closely, was not one thing but exploded brilliantly away in countless shards of sunshine that dared him to understand all that they illuminated. Molten, glowing, that light gave life to every living thing, it scorched the desert into being and it lit the world. It had no intelligence, just force that was happening too powerfully to care about the love and madness below. Nothing mattered to it, least of all the squalid streets of Suerte. The sun decided the destinies of men and women in million foot flames. It scorched the earth and shuttered cities. Lustre's little life was not even in the sun's awareness. It could kill him and not know it. Nor would Pedro in his dog's halo be missed except by other infinitesimal boys like him, like Lustre. For a moment, Lustre saw something beyond what he would ever know: Universes upon universes, rabbitholes rupturing out to infinity, Janus-faced deities, gods and devils, star-lit and sun-washed space, plantations of mountains and metropolises, clouds bursting into oceans, over islands, fire and flowers. Each sun floated in its fatherhood, creator lord over so many earths, so many children. He saw his living father, the sun, in light shower and turning shadow above the desert and above the city and he, little dark child inside the illumination, he saw life and he saw death: Each thing, animals, plants, others, all mirrored the life of the sun above them. And in the flit of an eye, the beat of a bass drop, the sun turned against some of the things of the earth and its natural thoughtless rotation let their life go dark and disposed of them.

SHARONE

Sharone couldn't find Lustre, not at night. The boy could hide in a spotlight so Sharone tried not to worry about his whereabouts. He didn't want to think about what mess Lustre might be in or what stress that mess was putting on his momma's mind. Sharone felt for the boy and for the boy's friend who had been shot. But Lustre would have to learn for hisself that there was no such thing as *Law and Order: San Suerte*. Murders rarely resulted in arrests, let alone much more than that, especially if they looked any-way gang-related and all you needed for that to be the case was blacks and Mexicans doing the dying. An attempt murder on a suspected gang member would disappear from law enforcement concern as easy as Eddie could disappear and reappear and go away again if he felt like it.

Instead of worrying his head over youngblood, Sharone searched his mind and then the cable channels for something easy, something simple, something, somewhere where he could escape, and, like a prayer answered after enough channel-surfing, there it was, television church, black television church no less with a lights-camera-action preacher to boot. The man was turning this way and that on the stage, liable to start breakdancing as he testified about the Book of Revelation, about Jesus returned burnished bronze and burning bright, about the pale horse, about the 144,000 souls and the slain little lamb.

(The sermon notwithstanding) lambs, Sharone figured, had been slain on a regular basis since the beginning of time and in countless number. Cain, he reflected, was an innocent knowing nothing of murder until he had committed it and stood in the sunlit field above his brother's dead body. The first murder brought death into the world. And from then on, nothing could be as before. Life had its limit. The future did not exist. There was no day but today to be redeemed.

Sharone sank further into the couch, dreading the pain in the small of the left side of his back that would come later. But he was too tired to do anything except sink and think. He had a big, imposing frame and two hands that in a fight would knock most men sideways, but that didn't matter in the end. He was as vulnerable as a woman at the hands of a bad man. He knew this from being taken: One night when he was still living the life he lived before this life, a thief had got the jump on Sharone, put the brother on the wrong side of a revolver, made him kneel and beg for his life, made him come out of his shoes and socks, made him strip naked in the dark under a freeway overpass and hand over his unsold wet weight like a burnt offering. Sharone still saw himself, still truly defined himself in these broken moments where all his strength was dissolved and he trembled naked in the breach.

He wanted to be a believer, maybe he did believe in the God that the television preacher spoke of, but he did not trust the book in the man's hand, not to mention all the other untrustworthy books of truth that religion and incarceration had brought his way. He read them scriptures alright, but always he found himself testing their truth against the truth he had already lived. A book was just a book, after all. It would never be life, but only what people chose to write and what they chose to remember and what they chose to make disappear. Whole religions had disappeared in fire, all their books piled up and burnt to lost ashes, so as far as Sharone was concerned redemption could only come in the present world, in this time and place, not from knowing no book.

Because he came from suffering people who still feared God, Sharone had listened intently when his jailhouse brothers would start talking about going to the mosque and about the intricacies of Nation of Islam doctrine. But he could never get down with the way their scripture, or at least what they told him about their scripture, seemed to license men, placing them superior over women. He had known that mind state already and knew not to visit it again.

The first house of worship he went to after incarceration was Reverend-City Councilman Sherwood's Baptist church, which persisted like an invalided elder in the neighborhood. Sharone knew it well so he went there, only to find that he knew it too well to stay. The church's ways, once he saw them from the inside, grew worrisome within the space of that single service: Sharone hated how the ushers passed the hat every fifteen minutes and he hated how Sherwood talked on and on about how thinking was not so important, but simply a vessel for haughty pride, how the mind's reasoning needed to be put to the side before one could be raptured away. All Sherwood counseled the parishioners to do was give up their money and pray and be and be and pray. It was the absence of thought that had gotten Sharone caught up and messed up in the first place. He didn't need Sherwood's preaching on how not to think.

He found his way to a Buddhist temple in a suburb a few towns over and on a typical wind-beaten, arid Wednesday night he sat down in a too-small-for-his-size, hard-backed chair amongst a congregation (he knew no other word for a religious gathering) of white people with their hair bees-wax woven into dreadlocks, and there he meditated for thirty-five minutes. Outside he could hear the river rush of traffic from the freeway and the wind whistling above and an occasional human voice. The meditation leader tolled a bell that began the meditation and from time to time the man would tell them not to think, just breathe: In-breath; out-breath; no thought. Sharone had identified a trend, but he complied as well as he could. He actually did try to still his mind. But it kept working and wandering—Sharone had too much on his mind just to be, in-breath, out-breath. When he tried to center himself in the breath, floating on the depthless, timeless simplicity of each escape and return of air, his center fell apart and he dropped like in a sudden falling dream into deep caves and dark downward shoots of memory and feeling and pain. There, in the descent, he saw his history in a million flitting panels full of chaos. Each memory snapped open and closed and he fell further and further through all of his past.

There, amongst all his tragedies he saw the one memory that he had tried to unremember. The crime for which he had never stood trial. The crime that had chased him to jail and had chased him away from trouble ever since: Back when he was hustling, inside a ramshackle dope house on a nameless Los Angeles street, a girl had come in off the track. Her arms were pockmarked, her eyes hid deep inside swollen lids. She was looking for protection, a pimp, Sharone remembered. But that might not even have been the case. It was too easy to tell himself that she had already been turned out. He watched as the boys whom he considered his friends vied for who would pimp her. He knew where this was going and he said nothing, did nothing despite the fact that he knew in his heart of hearts that whatever the girl wanted was not what she would get. That in fact when which-ever boy took her, gave her drugs, put her on the street and broke her down, that she would be way worse off than if she simply went homeless. Sharone remembered her dead, unconsenting, unobjecting eyes which he tried to meet, but that just stared indifferently back at him. He left out of there as quick as he could and quiet as it was kept.

And as soon as he was out the door, he tried to forget that the girl even existed.

When the meditation teacher finally tolled the bell to end the session, Sharone heaved out a breath that was anything but free. He knew he was nowhere near non-thought. The teacher explained that next there would be a ten-minute break for light refreshments, pastries and tea, through the open door at the far end of the center. Where everyone else seemed to take a minute to gather themselves and leave the meditative moment, Sharone rose like Easter morning and made for the back exit.

Despite himself, he commenced to meditate on his own time. Sharone didn't like to meditate, didn't enjoy the stillness or how terrifyingly sharp and deep all his thoughts cut as he sat alone in his bedroom on the floor and he especially hated seeing the girl in the dopehouse in his thoughts where for so long he had been able to hide from her. But he appreciated the way he felt after the meditation was over and he was full of fatigue. It was a relief to feel that he had survived his mind, his history, his sin, himself.

He heard tell that the Ethiopians meditated for four hours unbroken without a meditation teacher to ring any bell or point them to the refreshments room. There was an Ethiopian Tewahedo Orthodox Christian church on the East Side of San Suerte across the street from a popular check-cash outlet. He recalled, even as a child, being struck by the untroubled gracefulness, the upright dignity, the godly proud blackness of the parishioners as they filed in neat rows from off the squalid ghetto street into their place of holy worship. They were just so many smartly dressed children, no older than him but so much more dignified in dress and demeanor and every-other way, too; so many white-head-wrapped women; so many decoratively robed, stone-serious men. He remembered the colors, the red, the black, the green and yellow of the church front. But he could not recall ever wanting to attend service or even wanting to steal a glance inside.

Now, he decided to attend: He asked around and eventually found an Ethi girl who was not too shy of him. She had big, doe eyes and a round, moon-shaped face that belied her thin, small stature. She told Sharone that she could not sit beside him, but she could tell him how to dress properly, perfect white linens that floated on his skin like doves over darkness, and how to enter the church in such a way that people would either assume he was a newly arrived immigrant— or maybe a single man come down from Oakland or west from Phoenix—or possibly an American-born black man disillusioned by the white man's Christianity who found himself in search of the true first Word of God.

Inside, he sat in the very last row, where small, hard-back chairs took the place of pews. The crowd had overwhelmed the pews. With his height, he was able to sit still and look out over the several hundred smaller statured Ethiopians. There was a choir and singing, which reminded him of the black church, except the language and rhythm of the songs was completely different, high and wholly melodic, rocking him into a trance-state. Incense burned, the smoke filling the church like so much syrup, risen and settled, thick-sweet and still, holding him in its cloud until it was an even bet whether he would fall out in sleep or see God in the sweet smoke. The only reason he didn't do either was that the choir director repeatedly interrupted the song, calling things to a halt when even one singer fell off key.

The first hour of meditation was no different from the scatter-brained session Sharone had experienced at the Buddhist temple, no different from the welter of ideas that characterized his late-night, pre-bed ritual. The second hour he began to think about why he was thinking so much and this line of thought, which was longer and deeper than he'd expected, carried him well into the third hour. His mind felt like a state champion quarter-miler in full stride as he overtook the top of the arcing oval of the track and fled for the backstretch. He had been thinking hard for more than two hours continuously, but his mind was still in full, dry-mouthed, breathless sprint. It had exhausted memory and grievance and the dopehouse, and now it regarded the future, every hope and fear he had, but also wild theories beyond anything he had ever thought before. What if the Ethiopians sold their religion like the American Christians did, putting it in politicians' mouths and on talk radio? What then? What if this incense that was so far up his nostrils it had probably taken home in his brain by now, was actually a potion or the body of Christ or the aura of the Holy Ghost? What then? And what if Destiny made up her mind that she was in love with him and only him? What then? Would he have to tell her about the girl in the dopehouse when she did what women do and asked him to tell her everything? By the fourth hour, his mind and body had stilled. The future exhausted, there was nothing left in his mind but to remind himself to breathe, to circulate the one thing that would keep this completely used-up shell that he had transformed into alive.

The clothes he had worn that day smelled like the Ethiopians' incense for weeks afterward. His whole experience of the Tewahedo Church was like that: Engulfing, unrelenting. Its effect didn't die, didn't even dissipate. And he was not sure that he could go back until the shock of actually being rendered mindless, bodiless, a flawlessly opened vessel, finally wore off.

He kept making plans to return and worship with the Ethiopians. The girl, Addis, seemed disappointed in him when he did not come back. She stopped talking to him. Meanwhile, word must have gotten around amongst the Africans and the appropriative black Americans that there was a reformed ex-convict brother who was searching for his salvation. A group of Afrikan mystics down from Oakland got a hold of him for a week, inviting him to an abandoned warehouse where they put him through their paces. Orisha rites was how he would think of it later. That was the wrong name for what he witnessed, but that was the only language he had for such mysteries. A consecrated cast iron pot filled with ash, sticks and earth and items Sharone had no interest in investigating became the fetish, held aloft, questioned and praised and sung to and fallen before like it was God hisself. Sage and marijuana was burnt and Sharone lived in a haze of herbs for three days. Time and logic blurred. He wasn't sure how long the ceremonies lasted or even what each ritual was purposed toward. On the third day, he began to hallucinate: He saw the spiritual leader take a rabbit out of a box and hold it in his cupped hands like a sacrament. Prayers to the spirits left behind on the other side of the Atlantic rose like amens in church, with the same inflections, just different names given them, and the dark priest set the rabbit on the ground and another man held it still, and then the priest produced a long blade and swiftly beheaded the animal. Its blood gushed out onto the dank steel floor as it flailed the life out of itself, dead but unreconciled. Sharone felt one with the animal, saw his own head severed, his own body forcibly transitioned into a place after life and unclaimed by death. There was drumming and screaming and singing and ecstatic lulls that took him into the dead, exhausted pits of his despair . He was back in his bunk in the County jail and his bedsheet had become a woman. He felt its stickiness, the aftermath of his desire, and he was ashamed. If he had been fucking her, cumming in the filthy cloth, that would be one thing; but instead she was holding him, rocking him in her embrace like she would a child, and he knew that he was nothing more than a child and very frightened. He knew he was definitely not built for a long stay in jail, let alone prison. He realized, then, his sensitivity and his mortality and his eyes down, shamefaced fear. He was nineteen years old.

It was all closing in then, all the walls that were his life. But before they could take him back to Oakland or Africa or into those ocean waves, Sharone's homegrown black churchiness simply rose up and called him back from the mysteries of his hallucination. It had little to do with biblical Christianity, for he had decided that the bible was just another book, full of wisdom in its teachings, but in the end holding no final truth. No, it was just his blackness, his simple need for the still ground of his religious home, passing the hat and all that crap— that alone and nothing more held him in San Suerte and would not allow him, after all that searching, to be swept up in fuck and starlight and godly animism.

Sharone figured the birds would start chirping soon. It was past time for him to go to bed. Working a ball of indigestion down his throat and into his stomach, he raised himself from the clutches of the couch cushions and his own stasis and he stood for a moment, appreciating that his muscles moved at all for their careless owner. And then he knelt and prayed to a God he had not met.

Sharone was attracted to Destiny, but it went deeper than that. He knew what being orphaned did to a child. Destiny hadn't done the crimes that he had, nor had she turned away from a crime and let it take place like he did, but she was ungrounded and light-bodied as every child let loose, liable to be lost in the wind just like him.

It took a long time for them to even acknowledge to themselves, let alone to one another that they were more than two people who shared a small home in a dying neighborhood in a dead city. They both had their brief dreams, thoughts that flew through their minds and went out as fast as stove flames turned down. But it took time. And it took things transpiring; Eddie never making good on his promise, Sharone making good on his, Destiny listening to Ms. Little when she told the girl what a good brother Sharone truly was, even if he could only help her control her child but so much.

Lost in the wind, and then found and lost again, Lustre appeared to them and disappeared and reappeared and left them without warning and returned to them without reason.

Destiny and Sharone had to work their way through the furtive first moments and then the nights where they waited up for one another, only to have nothing meaningful to say after that key turned in its lock and the door opened on to the desired other. It required that they reach out of their private prisons, where their feelings were cased up like so many untouched stones and that they risk the openness and fragility that love brought dangerously with it. Both knew what it was to love a parent and to see that woman, that man disappear. They knew that love could start full and open and become a tomb where you could feel wind rushing through like your body had been hollowed and your heart opened to let the cold in. It was hard for them to get beyond their fears.

They made surprised, frightened, then slower, easier, deeper love one night and fell asleep together wrapped in each other's limbs on the floor between the couch and the television. Later, they awoke shivering. "That fan feels like rain falling on me," Destiny said. "And a hard wind blowing over us," Sharone added. He rose to a squat and scooped her up in his arms. "Before we catch the same cold," he said. She curled herself into a perfect coil inside the bed of Sharone's grasp and let herself be carried back to his bedroom. They were under the covers before they realized how easy and natural it was to sleep together.

Sharone spun the dial station to station as he drove his pizza delivery route. From being born and raised in the little city, he knew Suerte in such detail, every back road and alleyway dead end, that when he took the job he discovered that he didn't even need to think about addresses to find the homes where MapQuest's color-coded coordinates directed him. There was the radio to occupy him; the pirated frequencies with their underground hip-hop; the old rock and R&B songs on the major stations that he knew all the words to even though he didn't know who the singers were who sung them or even what the songs were called.

"Here's the question of the hour," the DJ's voice zinged out. "Is it your responsibility to tell your wife/husband/girlfriend/boyfriend every dirty little detail of your past? What if you slept with one of your wife's co-workers back in the day before you two ever met? What if that co-worker turns out to be her second cousin?"

"Oh, you gotta tell her about that," the co-host, a woman with a voice like an eighteen-year-old, chimed in.

"No, you don't!" the DJ shot back.

Then he fielded a caller's opinion and decided whether he approved of it or not.

Sharone drifted across lanes on the quiet residential road and neared the delivery destination, a suburban home flanked by a garden of cacti and piles of glitter-glazed rocks arranged into pathways criss-crossing the front yard. It was times like this that Sharone remembered how two-sided his town was. Back in the van, the DJ was protesting against his co-host and all the callers, who were all female: "You need to play the odds. The odds are, you're not gonna get caught so keep your damn mouth shut. She won't find out. If she does, it'll only mess up your relationship. And for what? The truth about something that's over anyway?"

Something about the cut of the man's laughter, about the way he tossed it out so carelessly in between his claims, like he might toss another person out of his way just as easily. Sharone changed stations, turning to the region of pirated frequencies between 1300 and 1500 on the dial. This felt like more honest territory. He checked the next address: The delivery route ran up into the groves like usual. He breathed in, let his wind settle in his stomach, and thought about how to tell Destiny about his true crime.

Sharone was nothing like Eddie. Destiny had known that all along, but now that they were in a relationship it mattered in particular ways. Sharone had no big visions, no dreams to make a million dollars in one fell swoop. And she liked that about him. As far as Destiny could tell, all Sharone wanted was to do right by folk and maybe find something he could call God. She did worry about him, though. Sometimes he had a look in his eyes at night that frightened her because it wasn't just that lost look that she could as well see in the mirror as in him, it was something more than that: Nights, something very sad flickered in Sharone's eyes. It was those flickers that caused her to wonder if something deeper didn't trouble him. But she loved his cooking and she appreciated his kind ways, the softness with which he dealt with her, his gentleness toward her, his truthful plainness, his sincere guardedness, and the way he exposed himself even more slowly than she did.

He looked at her in that troubled way one night and she didn't know what was different this time, whether it was that the moon was yellow and full, a gigantic cat's eye in the sky, or that she felt herself falling irrecoverably in love with him and needed to know whether to stay or go the other way, but she decided she should just ask him. "Sharone?"

"Um-hmm. What's up?"

"I just wanna know all there is to know about you, Sharone. That's not a crime."

She realized only after she'd said it that her choice of words was an incitement.

"I didn't kill no one."

"I was banking on that, honey." She peeled a smile out of herself, but he was scaring her now.

"Ain't nothin to do with no murder, but you won't want shit to do with me after you hear what it is."

"What is it?"

"It's bad," he said, "jus ain't no murder."

She backed into a chair and bent down to sit, knowing that she did not want to hear what would come next.

And then he proceeded to tell her about that night in Los Angeles. He told her about the girl in the trap house. He told her that she did not say much other than that she needed a pimp. That her face was a dead, expressionless mask. That he was too much of a coward to admit to himself what he knew about her, that she did not want to be there, that she did not want a pimp, that whatever she actually wanted she would not say because the right to that want had been taken from her. He knew she was scared, but that her face didn't say it because somehow the right to fear them had been taken from her, too. And he knew what would happen to her not in a year or a month but in that dopehouse that very night. That he chose those boys over that girl and left her to whichever one of them, or all of them. "I got ghost," he confessed. "Just lied and said I had a buyer pressin me so I could cut out."

He let that settle for a second and when she just sat there, he told her about another dark room full of people he did not actually know, the Santerias from Oakland. He told her about calling after the ancestors and how, for him, the ancestors were simply him as a child, his child-self, a god that was gone. He told her about how the priest brought out the rabbit and cut its head clean off, blood flooding everywhere. He told her how the rabbit didn't die right off, or it died still deathwalking around, headless but unsurrendered to the priest's work. He told her that he had felt merged with the creature, suspended between life and death, and that that sight had put him some-way in mind of the girl left behind in the dopehouse. He tried to lie to himself that he had never even seen her, that she did not exist, when in reality she was merging with and entering him, taking him. There was no leaving her. She was with him, inside of him, and every time he told himself anything else about himself it was only a lie.

That night Destiny left. Sharone waited up for her to return as if she were just out on a date or a company dinner. But he knew not just deep down, but up high, and all over, that she hadn't been dating anybody except him and that there was no company to dine with;

she had left him. He wished she would have argued, fallen on him in screams and cries and blows and blood, rather than this pure sudden absence.

He found himself unable to sleep and stayed wakeful and alert into the morning. But of course she did not come back.

At six a.m., he shoved off to work, as exhausted by his regret as any privation brought on by lack of sleep. He decided against calling Des or going to look for her. She was probably gone for good, he admitted to himself, at some point in the afternoon. He was in love with her and wanted to be with her, but he also knew that she was right to leave him. It was best she know everything about him and that she leave now before anything very serious happened between them. It was best not to have any secrets.

On the third day, the third evening, Lustre returned. Sharone knew he must look worse than usual when the boy asked "You OK, Sharone?" When he was supposed to be looking out for youngblood, not the other way around.

"I cain't tell you to forgive that boy, Lustre. Eddie's his name? You gots to resolve that shit how you see fit, but promise me this one thing: Don't you let let his shadow follow you forever. Promise me that."

"I promise," Lustre said.

Sharone didn't believe him, but he had no ground to tell anyone what to do. He let it be.

And later, when he excused himself and went to the restroom, Sharone heard the apartment door click delicately closed and he knew that Lustre was gone. It didn't surprise him, and not just because the boy was magnetized by the same streets that had shot up his friend. Everyone was bound to leave, Sharone figured, for reasons good or bad, so the boy getting ghost wasn't but another vanishing thing. He waited up for nothing but eternity until an early sun rose in that still night, cresting a world that had yet to accept its light. Sharone watched its slow ascent. After a little while, the sky started to turn that first cold steel blue that unveiled Suerte's palm trees tall and brooding and windblown as movie stars. It revealed, westerly, the plaza's stunted construction, and it brought into focus the Adventist church steeple, the Party Doll bar's Elvis and Marilyn graffiti, and the tattoo parlor with the big mural of the sister in tight jeans and halter top that confessed her form from her hips to her waist to her bare arms sleeved with masks laughing and crying. The sun met the desolate downtown, the vacant lots, the old, shut-down Carousel Theater, the Cesar Chavez statue, and the state flag fluttering at full mast. It illuminated the memorial to McDonald's and the check-cash joints and the abandoned boxing gym and the Central City Mission and Mount Vernon and G Street and La Raza Liquor and the freeway overpasses that triangulated and cordoned a community. The barrios lit up and the roosters that the Mexicans still woke with came alive crowing in full throat, and Sharone was certain she would never come back. He did not trespass the bedroom that had been hers of recent as much as his even though, technically, it was all his if it was anyone's alive. She was just the sub-letter, he told himself. But he knew title and deed was just a fiction when you were in love. The bedroom had become more than a contracted space—it had opened wide upon his heart and he couldn't close it. The lease didn't tell the half when it came to what she meant to him.

But there was no way she was coming back, and no way to justify going to get her. He wouldn't ask her to forgive a white man for dragging and lynching a black man, or for letting it happen, so why should she forgive him? She had left because she did not want to live with a man who could do what he had done. Or she had left because forgiveness, that Jesus forgiveness, that Mandela forgiveness, was only doable at a distance. Scripture said to turn the other cheek, not curl up under the covers with him. There were limits to compassion.

In the end, it was as simple and as complicated as losing Destiny.

When Destiny did come back, later that day, she was subdued. She nodded at Sharone but did not speak. She went into the bedroom, where her things waited for her like spring flowers born too early, stunted by winter ground. She closed the door behind her. He watched her disappear and then went and sat on the couch and turned on the television. Better to distract hisself than to obsess about what she was bound to do. He was not sure what he would do when she started to carry the heavy things out and he knew he should help and that he shouldn't at the same time.

But the door did not open. He charted the time between commercials and after fifteen minutes he knew that things were not going as he had figured they would. She wasn't leaving, at least not very quickly.

After an hour, he had no idea what to think. He had resigned himself that she wanted nothing to do with him. But the fact that she had, without a word, gone in the room and was laid-up in there soundless and undeparting threw him off.

Eventually, she opened the door a little and called for him. "Sharone?"

"Des?"

The television program continued to drone in the background.

"Sharone."

"Yeah?"

"Please turn off the TV. And come here," she said. Her voice was soft but directing.

He did as he was told.

When he entered the bedroom that was his and hers and no one's all at once, she was lying still on top of the bare mattress. Her body was splayed like the cross. The sheets had been flung on the ground, a dirty white moat between them. She did not look at him, just lay there staring at the ceiling.

"Sharone?"

He didn't answer. Standing in the doorway, he had fallen beyond expectation into an opening where anything was possible, disgrace and rebirth, the end and the beginning, and everything else besides.

"Sharone, is this how she was?"

Fear, latent, rose immediate inside him. He knew what Des was asking, but didn't want to know it, let alone answer her on it.

"Tell me," she pressed. "Show me how she was when y'all niggas did what they did."

It was a long minute before he could even move. When he did, he came slowly into the bedroom that seemed not in the least his now, that was under the ownership of that girl whose name he never even troubled to know.

"I dunno," he said cautiously, lamely.

Destiny rose up on the bed, balancing on her haunches. "Yes, you do."

He remembered the way the poor girl's shirt rode up over her stomach, not above her breasts but high enough to expose her laddered ribs. He remembered thinking that if them boys ran a train that the girl's jeans would crumple around her ankles like a smashed soda can.

"When I was there," he said, "they was jus, people's clothes was on. She was standin there like you standin there now."

"You were afraid they were gonna do something to her with her clothes off? See, Sharone, ain't no way she coulda stood like I'm standing now without no power. You knew what them niggas was

74

about to do. You admitted that to me already. So, the only question is what would you do now if she was right here and y'all had her like she was in this room right here? What would you do now?"

He took in as much air as he could.

"What would you do, Sharone?"

"I dunno," he said again, this time telling the truth. He didn't know how he would react now except that he would not leave. But what did that even mean? That he would stay and witness the shit, or be brought even deeper into whatever it was that happened. He knew what happened. He knew from seeing her in the streets days, weeks, months later, turning tricks, getting skinny. But if he went up and did something for her, pulled her away, threw her over his shoulder to rescue her, the boys in that dopehouse would only take him for a renegade gorilla pimp and beat both of them down. There was no way the two of them were getting out of that room—at least not looking and walking and talking like nature intended.

"Why you dunno?" She mocked his mumbling. "You've had how many years to think about it? Ten?"

It was true, he had had ten years and his answers were as weak as ever. The answer was that every answer was a dead end. The real problem was that she was there in the first place and that he had been there that night faced with that decision in the first place. "I wanna say," he began, "that I'd help her. But that's pro'ly not true."

He gazed at Destiny. It was getting to where it wasn't even an effort of imagination to envision the Los Angeles girl in her place and to imagine the entire scene, all those people, crowded into this little room. "If I were to try to help her, we'd both be in for some trouble. Wadn't no helpin at that point."

Destiny brought her hand to her face and wiped at what he took for tears. She said nothing.

"I coulda saved myself, or I coulda tried to save her—" He struggled for the proper words, but there were none.

She looked at him with eyes that were just as searching, just as unreconciled. Then, crazy, awkward, betrayed, she swiped at him open-handed, long-nailed, scraping his face. Sharone didn't see it coming and took the blow flush. His skin stung worse than the pain from the angriest wasp and he felt something liquid running down the side of his face. Long after the time of her anger had passed and she had retreated to a far corner of the room, trembling, staring at him, Sharone stayed where she left him. He stared back at her, but there was nothing there anymore just like how when the girl in Los Angeles looked to him, looked right at him, her gaze fixed with his, searching him out as if to ask if he were any different than these others and he just stood there and stared back there had been nothing in her eyes but his own dead image staring back at him. He had walked away and left her there so that he would not have to see her, or what would happen to her, and because he believed that he could hide from himself. But there was no hiding: He saw in Destiny's eyes the boy that he thought he had buried inside himself reflected back at him and he knew he was not a new man.

They stared at each other for a long time, he and Destiny. There was blood on his cheek and on her hand. They didn't move. After a while, Sharone could no longer hear himself breathing and he knew the terrible rush inside of him was slowing. He grew calmer. Destiny's breath dropped out of the range of hearing, too, and he saw something calm but cold come into her eyes. "I saw Lustre on G Street as I was coming back over here," she said. "You need to go clean up before he walks in all unannounced like you know he's bound to. I'ma be in here." She waved her hand around the room.

Sharone listened to his slowing, calming heart and nodded yes, for Lustre. In a way he felt alive for the first time in ten years and it was all for that child. He turned and walked out, leaving the room to Destiny for as long as she would want it.

"Sharone," she called from over his shoulder so that he had to stop and turn and look at her.   "Don't ask for me."

HOME

Lustre Little got to where he could go days, then weeks, then forever never thinking about Eddie Richard, about what the streets said Eddie had done to Lustre's friend to get his shine. After a while, with Eddie out the picture, what use was it wondering who did what? Paid was never going to get better. Lustre realized that. Lustre would go visit his friend and Señora Velasquez in their shabby little apartment in the barrio. Removing the crime from his mind did not remove the victim.

Lustre would knock on the door and Señora Velasquez would slide up in her slippers so loud he could hear their every fiber splitting. She would open the door and wait for him to raise his white T-shirt, his purple and gold knock-off Laker jersey, his old black bomber jacket to where she could see the waistband of his shorts or khakis: No armas.

"Gracias, mijo," she would say, nodding, not bothering to pat him down. "Thank you."
Then she would gesture that he come inside and he would kneel next to her and they would pray together, their knees grinding into the hard tile floor. They prayed and prayed and Paid sat there in silence in his wheelchair inside his halo.

After Señora Velasquez rose, ending that ritual, Lustre would sit down on the rigid plastic sofa cover. He tried to pretend he was not uncomfortable. But the whole situation was, of course, uncomfortable. Paid, Pedro rarely made a sound, but the plastic sofa cover talked non-stop. It squeaked and blurted and scratched and when it was done vocalizing, it creased Lustre's pants. Lustre could spend two, three hours rearranging his ass on the damn thing and still it tormented him. He had no idea why anyone, let alone every Latino and three quarters of the black community in San Suerte would inconvenience themselves this much just for the sake of a clean sofa. It was not his place to object, though.

The sofa cover was the kind of thing that had not bothered Lustre so much in the years that he haunted the Velasquez home before Pedro was shot. The sofa covers were nothing new and he had never liked them one bit. Now, though, they took on devilish qualities with each visit to the Velasquez home. The discomfort radiated from the furniture to Lustre, Pedro and Pedro's mother, becoming inescapable. There were no conversations to be had with his friend; yes, Pedro would pipe up and speak now and again, say something to his mother, but the inspiration was always lost quickly and then it was back to the silent contemplation of fate, of violence, of a world without redemption. Pedro lilted in and out of consciousness. He drooled on himself sometimes and Señora Velasquez had to come behind him like the mother of a two-year-old and wipe him clean. Sometimes Lustre even found himself mothering his friend, cleaning his halo, wiping food and filth from his cheeks, his lips, his neck, his shoulders.

These were difficult visits and, because of the difficulty and awkwardness and sadness of it all, Lustre never said much to Señora Velasquez either—what was there to say?

Is he getting better? I'm sorry, he is not. *How is your day going?* Not good, mijo. *Why do you insist on this stupid fucking plastic sofa cover?*

Thank the Lord for television. The three of them could sit and watch shows for hours. Pedro wasn't the only one who would drift in and out of consciousness. Each of them lost consciousness periodically, especially after meals of mole and rice and beans; they lolled, necks off-kilter like beheaded prisoners, and drooled on themselves while asleep and muttered dark, primitive things. They lost their wherewithal and their dignity and awoke stained and disoriented. As the coma lifted, Lustre would come to a spittled mess, the TV volume set to high would blare at him, usually a Telemundo game show with a big-bosomed white Mexican woman invading eardrums about something that meant nothing. But it didn't matter, game shows, baseball scores, the news of the day's dead in the wars in Afghanistan and Iraq, it all gave him the same sick, sad feeling. He knew that this was how it ended for most people, propped up in front of their television in a dimly lit room. This was how it would obviously end for Pedro, and probably for himself, too—one day many decades or a matter of days from now, in the dark, while the trifling world blazed so bright, all glamoured-up and packaged for sale. Lustre did not think about the shining things on the screen. In that dark home, Lustre saw the sun, the living god, and he knew what it was to be alive raw and broken and he became a man.

reading guide

Theme: COMING OF AGE

Lustre is, in part, the coming of age story of the novella's main character, the eponymously named teenage boy, Lustre. Lustre learns a lot throughout the course of the story despite adults intentionally keeping much information from him.

- Write a scene where an adult intentionally withholds important information about the past from a child or adolescent.

- Write a scene where a child or adolescent learns something that is vitally important.

Bonus question:

- *Lustre* learns different things from his mother (Ms. Little), Sharone, and Destiny. Who in your life have you learned the most from and did you learn from what they told you or from observing them?

Theme: REBEL WITH A CAUSE

Lustre also features Destiny Deveraux, who is an orphan, a bad student, and a pretty good rebel.

- Discuss some of the advantages and disadvantages of being rebellious in school and in society.

Theme: LOCATION x 3

Lustre is set in San Suerte, an economically stratified ex-urb in the California desert, far from any major city.

- What are some of the features of the city or town where you live and how would you describe it? Try describing your hometown or a place you've lived in three different ways:

    o Describe the place using only factual details;
    o Describe the place using only sensory details and images; and
    o Describe the place using symbolism and metaphor.

Theme: TYPES OF NARRATIVE

Lustre does not follow a traditional redemptive narrative arc.

- Make a list of common narratives (i.e., boy-meets-girl, prodigal son story, etc.).
- Discuss some of the problems that you perceive in these common, or traditional, narratives.
  - Discuss how you might disrupt a common narrative with your own narrative.

Theme: SOCIAL COMMENTARY

Lustre depicts people struggling to overcome or escape several major social problems.

- Think about a crisis of great social importance. How might you engage the issue to bring greater social awareness to it?
  - Through social media? Through a speech? Through a story?
    - ► What are the advantages and disadvantages of each medium?
- Think about ironic representation versus blunt, powerful representation. Discuss how writers use irony to portray critical social issues.

Theme: NATURE AND SYMBOL

The sun has great significance in the novella.

- Think about the natural world. What five objects in the natural world do you think have held the most symbolic and spiritual significance for human beings throughout time?
- Pick one object in the natural world and write about it from your perspective.
  - o Then write about it from the perspective of another person in the contemporary world.
    - ▸ Now write about it from the perspective of somebody from the past or the future.

acknowledgments

I began work on this novella many, many, years ago, so the list of my thank you's is potentially very long. I should first acknowledge the work that both my friend E.J. (many years ago) and my partner Duana (more recently) have done with me to make this a much better book than it would otherwise have been. I must also thank my writing group, Laleh, Joel, Muthoni, and Shanthi.

I need, too, to thank John Molina and Daniel Mendoza, both formerly of Goliad Press, this book's original home before pandemic-related financial difficulties delayed its publication and made an alternate plan of publication necessary. Finally, I must thank the visionary,

J. K. Fowler, founder of Nomadic Press, for giving *Lustre*, wayward child that it has been, a new and welcoming home and publishing it despite its numerous delays.

Keenan Norris

Keenan Norris's books include the novel *The Confession of Copeland Cane*, which won the 2022 Northern California Book Award, the book of essays *Chi Boy: Native Sons and Chicago Reckonings*, and the novel *Brother and the Dancer*, which received the 2012 James D. Houston Award. Keenan teaches at San Jose State University, where he is coordinator of the Steinbeck Fellows Program. In 2021, he served as a University of Virginia Rea Visiting Writer. His essays have appeared in *Alta*, *Los Angeles Review of Books*, and *Los Angeles Times*.

4 OTHER WAYS TO
SUPPORT NOMADIC PRESS WRITERS

Please consider supporting these funds. You can donate on a one-time or monthly basis from $10–∞ You can also more generally support Nomadic Press by donating to our general fund via nomadicpress.org/donate and by continuing to buy our books.

As always, thank you for your support!

Scan the QR code for more information and/or to donate.

You can also donate at nomadicpress.org/store.

ABOUT THE FUNDS

XALAPA
FUND

XALAPA FUND

The Xalapa Fund was started in May of 2022 to help offset the airfare costs of Nomadic Press authors to travel to our new retreat space in Xalapa, Veracruz in Mexico. Funds of up to $350 will be dispersed to any Nomadic Press published author who wishes to travel to Xalapa. The funds are kept in a separate bank account and disbursements are overseen by three (3) Nomadic Press authors and Founding Publisher J. K. Fowler.

Inherent in these movements will be cultural exchanges and Nomadic Press will launch a reading series based out of the bookstore/cafe downstairs from the space in August 2022. This series will feature Xalapa-based writers and musicians as well as open-mic slots and will be live streamed to build out relationships between our communities in Oakland, California, Philadelphia, Pennsylvania, and the greater US (and beyond).

EMERGENCY FUND

Right before Labor Day 2020 (and in response to the effects of COVID), Nomadic Press launched its Emergency Fund, a forever fund meant to support Nomadic Press-published writers who have no income, are unemployed, don't qualify for unemployment, have no healthcare, or are just generally in need of covering unexpected or impactful expenses.

Funds are first come, first serve, and are available as long as there is money in the account, and there is a dignity centered internal application that interested folks submit. Disbursements are made for any amount up to $300. All donations made to this fund are kept in a separate account. The Nomadic Press Emergency Fund (NPEF) account and associated processes (like the application) are overseen by Nomadic Press authors and the group meets every month.

BLACK WRITERS FUND

On Juneteenth (June 19) 2020, Nomadic Press launched the Nomadic Press Black Writers Fund (NPBWF), a forever fund that will be directly built into the fabric of our organization for as long as Nomadic Press exists and puts additional monies directly into the pockets of our Black writers at the end of each year.

Here is how it works: $1 of each book sale goes into the fund. At the end of each year, all Nomadic Press authors have the opportunity to voluntarily donate none, part, or all of their royalties to the fund. Anyone from our larger communities can donate to the fund. This is where you come in! At the end of the year, whatever monies are in the fund will be evenly distributed to all Black Nomadic Press authors that have been published by the date of disbursement (mid-to-late December). The fund (and associated, separate bank account) has an oversight team comprised of four authors (Ayodele Nzinga, Daniel B. Summerhill, Dazié Grego-Sykes, and Odelia Younge) + Nomadic Press Executive Director J. K. Fowler.

PAINTING THE STREETS FUND

The Nomadic Press Painting the Streets Fund was launched in February 2022 to support visual arts programs in Oakland flatlands' schools. Its launch coincided with the release of *Painting the Streets: Oakland Uprising in the Time of Rebellion*. Your donations here will go directly into a separate bank account overseen by J. K. Fowler (Nomadic Press), Elena Serrano (Eastside Arts Alliance), Leslie Lopez (EastSide Arts Alliance), Rachel Wolfe-Goldsmith (BAMP), and Andre Jones (BAMP). In addition, all net proceeds from the sale of *Painting the Streets: Oakland Uprising in the Time of Rebellion* will go into this fund. We will share the fund's impact annually on project partner websites. Here are a few schools that we have already earmarked to receive funds: Ile Omode, Madison High School, McClymonds High School, Roosevelt Middle School, Elmhurst Middle School, Castlemont High School, Urban Promise Academy, West Oakland Middle School, and POC Homeschoolers of Oakland.